TURKEYFOOT

ADVANCED PRAISE
TURKEYFOOT
by Rick Childers

"This harrowing debut is equal parts grit and empathy. ***Turkeyfoot*** is full of complex characters, pitch-perfect dialogue, and a sense of place so vibrant you can hear the birds singing, see the mist-shrouded hills, and smell the smoke of the off-brand cigarettes. Rick Childers is a writer who cares as deeply about language as he does about action, whose love for Appalachia shows clearly in his insistence on showing its joys, sorrows, and complications."
> —**Silas House**, New York Times Bestselling novelist and Kentucky Poet Laureate

"A story of place richly imagined, ***Turkeyfoot*** ties together a cast of characters fully fleshed and deeply scarred. Where Childers shines is in his understanding of the intimacy demanded by such places. Here, no one is ever more than one person removed. All are linked like bloodkin."
> —**David Joy,** author of ***Those We Thought We Knew***, winner of the Willie Morris Award and the Thomas Wolfe Literary Award

"Rick Childers brings to ***Turkeyfoot*** an ear for language, an eye for detail, and a feel for the structure of story that will keep the human face of the opioid epidemic before us."
> —**Michael Henson**, author of ***Maggie Boylan***

TURKEYFOOT

a novel

RICK CHILDERS

SHOTGUN HONEY
2024

TURKEYFOOT
Text copyright © 2024 **Rick Childers**

All rights reserved. This book or any portion thereof may not be reproduced or used in any manner whatsoever without the express written permission of the publisher except for the use of brief quotations in a book review.

This book is a work of fiction. Names, characters, places, and incidents either are products of the author's imagination or are used fictitiously. Any resemblance to actual persons, living or dead, events, or locales is entirely coincidental.

Published by **Shotgun Honey Books**

215 Loma Road
Charleston, WV 25314
www.ShotgunHoney.com

Cover by Bad Fido.

First Printing 2024.

ISBN-10: 1-956957-74-X
ISBN-13: 978-1-956957-74-7

9 8 7 6 5 4 3 2 1   24 23 22 21 20 19

For B.

TURKEYFOOT

*He made a pit, and digged it,
And is fallen into the ditch which he made.
His mischief shall return upon his own head,
And his violent dealing shall come down upon his own pate.*
—*Psalms 7:15-16*

Opium! dread agent of unimaginable pleasure and pain! I had heard of it as I had of manna or of Ambrosia, but no further how unmeaning a sound was it at that time! what solemn chords does it now strike upon my heart! what heart-quaking vibrations of sad and happy remembrances!
—*Thomas De Quincey*

CHAPTER ONE

Greedy, liar, crook, scum, cutthroat. Sweetie had been called it all, but it didn't bother him none. Most of the time it was just a junkie slinging mud.

Sweetie Goodins climbed up the small knobby mountain behind him and his father's house until he hit a cliff face. He had just turned seventy-one. His knees cracked and ached as he planted his boot for a foothold. The hill seemed steeper than when he was a boy. He sat down with his back against the sheer face of the cliff and the wind pawing at his cheeks from the west. His chest pounded as he caught his breath in shallow pulls of air. He arched his neck back until he was staring up the dark, gray wall that gave way at the top to a crumbling slope of moss and tree roots. He felt nauseous and closed his eyes, massaging his temples to focus back on the task before him.

Sweetie had been out hunting mushrooms. It was a hot day for May, but spring had come on just right for them. Even this late in the season he could still find cool shady spots where morels spawned. The leaves on the ground were damp from the morning dew. The sun rose and dripped back down into the hills. The thin canvas straps of his backpack had tugged against his shoulders each step up the hillside—he took it off now and laid it at his feet while he breathed slowly. In his back pocket he could feel the frame of a little black .22 pistol he kept for snakes.

After some time, the sun began to shine bright above, but it stayed dark under the canopy of poplar trees. Sweetie always noticed how on this side the leaves looked a darker shade of green. They matched the color of his eyes. Those eyes straight from his mother. A color like the river; familiar, comforting, but strong. Like something that had been and would always be.

Sweetie let his eyes wander and soon they worked over a tree line at the edge of a clearing. His father always said deer used to be thick on Turkeyfoot. Wasn't strange at all to find signs of rubbing. Told Sweetie he'd found two tangled up in death once, their antlers still locked together as they lay rotting in the dirt.

Such moments didn't last in Sweetie's life. The flip phone in his pocket cracked the silence around him with a chime. He sighed as he reached for it.

"Howdy," Sweetie said.

"I'm down here at the corner stop, Sweetie. I'm bad sick. Will you bring me a pill or two?" Case said.

On his way down from the woods the high sun licked at Sweetie's shoulders through the treetops. Slate rocks crumbled beneath his boots and the mud sucked at his heel each time he lifted to step again.

The gate to the farmhouse was chained closed. Chigger weeds had taken over the once-lush front yard. Water jugs lined the base of the house, stained yellow from years of use. His father would fill them to the brim with spring water only to empty them again.

"That Case Estes boy has been down at the corner store asking about you. He keeps calling the house and carrying on," his father said. The man sat on the porch whittling down the skinny end of a long crooked stick, one of the only tasks he cared to set his mind to since Sweetie's mother had passed on from this world. Just about the only thing he could manage at his age. The old man was nearly ninety. Sweetie's parents had reared him right here on this same mountain from the time they were only teenagers. It seemed like an ancient time as Sweetie tried to think of his two young parents. He scraped the mud from the bottom of his boots onto the edge of the porch and dropped his empty backpack at the top of the steps. He wiped his hands on the back of his pants and headed to his truck.

"You need anything while I'm down there?" he asked his father.

"Get me a bag of peppermints if they got any."

"They always do."

Sunshine or rain clouds, life was steady on Turkeyfoot Mountain. It was east of town, peaking right along the county line, a humble giant against the hazy Kentucky horizon. Sweetie eyeballed a stand of clouds blowing in as he slammed the door shut and the Chevrolet's engine cranked over into a thrum. He took off down the gravel road and turned out towards town, then he rolled his window down and felt the wind hit the side of his face. There was a drop in the road coming off the mountain where he could smell his brakes getting hot just before the pavement flattened back out and the steep banks turned to fields of hay at the bottom.

"Do you know where we are?" Sweetie's father would ask him when he was learning to drive their old Ford truck. He could still imagine the motion of clumsily shifting the three on the tree. It was one of his favorite memories of growing up in this place.

Turkeyfoot didn't seem like much to most outsiders. Another corpse of a town. But there was more to it for people like him who knew it before the bottom fell out. Used to be the railroad ran right through town, that's what drew a lot of folk for work, and other businesses followed the money. The trains had almost all but stopped for the most part. The city wanted to take tax dollars and open a type of historical center there about the railroad that once was. Sweetie never could see the sense in all that. Seemed better to let that old dog lie. Times changed, just the way it was. And besides, the railroad tracks were one of his favorite places to meet people wanting to buy dope since nobody hardly went out that way anymore. He had even poached a few deer out there towards the far end, late of the evenings. Wouldn't be anymore of that with a community center opening to bring buses of tourists in.

The gravel road adjacent to the train tracks ran a good piece each way. More than once he'd told someone like Case just to meet him down there under the bridge where the railroad and the river hugged up against one another. Those were the three things that ran through Turkeyfoot: the railroad, the river, and dope. Lots of dope. Whether it was FDA approved and scripted out by a doctor, or whatever kind was being smuggled up by the Mexicans. He'd even seen more of the locally sourced ways of getting high. People wouldn't take the time to hunt agate rock or ginseng or mushrooms anymore, but they'd figure real quick on how to cook up some crystal.

It was pretty much pick your poison or your pleasure around Sweetie's hills. He had never seen anything like it in his life. He laughed to himself sometimes thinking of the way his old granny had fretted over all of them taking to whiskey and tobacco. Such seemed tame now. Everybody around him had been hollowed out from the inside. Sweetie had profited a good while off everyone's taste for these pills, but with the law cracking down and junkies turning snitch it was only a matter of time. Pretty soon the Mexicans and the trailer trash crazy enough to try their hand as cooks would have the market at their fingertips. The only thing Sweetie reckoned would never stop running through Turkeyfoot was the river. That broad, chugging Kentucky River. But there were days when he even questioned that.

The Happy-Top Corner Stop and Deli was the last pull off before getting into town. A single gas pump sat like a relic and rumor was that the fuel was watered down. Dusty gravel trailed into the road from people spinning tires on their way out. Sweetie saw Case as soon as he pulled into the corner store parking lot. The young man had a dirty John Deere hat pulled snug on his head, sweat stains climbing towards the crown of the cap, greasy curls of brown hair hanging at his shoulders. Case looked gnarled and twisted and ugly, like a knot on a log. Nothing like the scrawny kid that Sweetie remembered watching grow up down the road from him. As he rolled his window down, he thought to himself that Case wreaked like dog shit or catfish dough bait, a heavy stench that hit him like a sucker punch. A wrinkled denim button-down swallowed up the younger man's bony frame, more perspiration seeped from underneath his armpits. He spotted Sweetie, rolled out a laugh, and sucked on his cigarette as he waved towards the truck.

"Sweetie, man! I've missed you. What do you know?"

"Not much, Case. Just keeping busy up at the house. You know how it goes."

Down off the mountain, the day was covered by a hot, sticky blanket of air. So thick even the birds were smothered in it. Across the street from the corner store a child chased a dog with a water hose.

"I've been thinking about the good old days, man. You remember how scared I used to get as a kid about that old oak tree above the house?" Case wiped his hands on his pant legs while he spoke. "When a storm came through and started rocking that old bastard, I just knew it was gonna come down on the lot of us. I'd crawl right up under the coffee table and hide. You remember that, Sweetie?"

"I sure do. You've always been kindly fool headed."

"You told me if anything it'd be like the firewood coming to us for a change. I'll never forget that." Case laughed and patted his kneecap. "You watched after me back then about as much as my parents did. Hell, more than they did—" Case stopped abruptly and Sweetie couldn't help but think that the boy's dark eyes looked more like a dog's than a man's.

"I was scared of the world back then. It ain't much to take in anymore," Case said.

"I guess not if you ain't got a straight head for it," Sweetie said.

"I don't know what's got into me lately. I just ain't got no damn gumption anymore, Sweetie. It's like it's all just been ripped up out of me. Ever last drop of gumption dried up and gone."

Case looked away from Sweetie. He took a drag so hard off a Kentucky's Best that Sweetie wondered if the cigarette would turn inside out.

"You know, sometimes I think I'd be better off a greasy spot on the road, somewhere for the crows to gather. Just ain't got a shred of gumption in me anymore." Case said.

Case looked put out. His greasy curls swayed as a stiff breeze passed through. His yellow teeth bit down on the soggy end of his cigarette. Sweetie knew when he saw the crumpled soft pack that Case was down on his luck. The only time he bought anything other than Marlboro was when he was broke or wild or both, which was most of the time nowadays.

"Whatever happened to that old tree out that way?" Case asked.

"I cut it down after y'all moved into town. Just a rotten old stump there now."

"An old rotten stump. I figure that's about as much a body could hope to leave. I'd just as soon lay down like one of them hills against the sky." Case didn't reach for another cigarette. His eyes stared across the road where the creamy blue sky mixed into a burning sunset. Thick peppered clouds spread out in gobs above them—it put Sweetie to mind of his mother's gravy. He had forgotten how long it had been since he'd had that gravy. He felt himself getting thirsty just looking at the clouds.

"Say, I could use one of them Percocet if you got any," Case said.

"I got a couple of small ones, but that's it. You got any money for me?"

"You know I'm always good for it."

Too many times Sweetie had heard those words uttered. Not only from Case but from all the people he fooled around with when it came to them pills. And not a single one of them was actually any good for it. He didn't have the time or energy to argue with Case today. He wanted to get home to his father and take a shower. Sweetie told Case to hop in his truck, where he took a Percocet out of his stash under the driver's seat. It was only a fifteen milligram, but Case didn't argue none. At least it'd keep him from getting sick until he could find another way to score. Sweetie told the younger man he had to get going and watched as the scarecrow-like figure took off stepping down the road towards town.

Sweetie eyed himself in the truck's rearview mirror. He had always been slender, but now his face seemed to droop. His hair, once black, had turned a darkened silver color like steel. He wore a stretched-out pocket tee that was still partially damp from his hike up the mountainside. Blades of grass were clumped to the bottom of his jeans and plastered to the toes of his work boots from mowing the yard earlier that day. As he stepped out of the truck the thick Kentucky air filled his nose; he tried to clear his throat to spit but couldn't muster anything.

Inside the corner store, Sweetie walked by a round-bellied woman with tattoos on her neck and up her arms. She stood in the back of the store fighting with the fountain drink dispenser and a toddler.

"Here now, get over here, Isaiah! Don't put that in your mouth!" she hollered.

Before Sweetie saw the boy, he heard the patter of bare feet against the greasy gas station floor. He was a chubby-cheeked kid with a head as round as a ball and a shine in his eye. A baby boy with hair as light as sunshine and deep blue eyes.

Sweetie grabbed a bag of hard candy for his father and got in line behind the tattooed woman. She was looking at the rows of scratch-off tickets behind a Plexiglas case.

The boy side-eyed Sweetie while they waited, his mother jabbering at the worn-out woman behind the register.

"Let me get eight of them Wild Aces. Even if we hit the jackpot, we decided his daddy ought to just serve the rest of his time up there at Three Forks."

Off to the side, a crusty young man and a whisper of a woman cursed back and forth at each other over cigarettes, neither of them a day over thirty. But even in their youth, they had those sunken eyes, a telltale sign to Sweetie that they were hooked on junk just as bad as Case or anybody else was.

A toy truck in his hand, the blue-eyed boy offered Sweetie a bucktooth grin. He smiled back.

"You ain't leaving the store with that, Isaiah! Put it back!"

His mother snatched the toy away and led him by the wrist out the door.

"Is that all for you, sir?" the clerk asked as Sweetie tossed the bag of peppermints onto the counter.

"That'll be it," Sweetie told the woman. Her hat with the gas station's logo sat perched on top of a greasy bun of brown hair. Sweetie couldn't see the knot of curls, but he'd known plenty of plumb-tired women just like her in his life. He handed her a crumpled-up twenty-dollar bill from his front pocket and waited as she made change.

"Have a good one," she muttered, already perking her ears towards the shaky couple. As Sweetie stepped back out into the evening air, they were asking the clerk for a pack of Pall Mall Blue. He had barely made it across the parking lot when he heard them behind him.

"You got any of those, Sweetie?" The crusty man hollered out before the gas station door had even slammed shut. Sweetie turned to face the two, unsure of what he should say. The woman's lips sank in around her gums where her teeth used to be.

"What did you say to me?" Sweetie asked.

"You got a thirty or anything? We heard you was cool."

"You must have me confused with someone else, dopeheads." Sweetie started back towards his truck, squeezing the bag of peppermints tight in his fist. He scanned the parking lot, opened his truck door, and hopped in the seat. The tattooed lady and the blue-eyed boy were long gone. There were no other vehicles besides his truck. The man and woman each lit a cigarette and sat down at a picnic table in front of the corner store. The heat of the day had started to fade, and he could hear the bugs chirping around him as the evening settled in.

CHAPTER TWO

A late dogwood was beginning to bloom in the front yard where the Perleys' driveway ended. Its white leaves popped against the surrounding green. Lucy Perley sat on the front porch steps picking at a scab on her shin. Her father's boots stuck out from underneath the broad front end of an Oldsmobile well beyond its prime. Sweat stung his eyes, and his hands shook while his fingers worked to unscrew the oil plug. He scooted around and reached for the drain pan but fumbled the plug. Black shimmering motor oil poured into his face and filled his mouth. He spat the warm sludge out into the gravel and cursed. John Perley kicked up dust trying to crawl out. When he stood up, he took the ratchet in his hand and dented in the fender of the car. He struck it until chips of paint flaked off and then slung the tool into the side of the trailer.

With a yard the sun always seemed to shine on, Lucy figured this world of hers was solid as packed dirt. Over a slight hill was her tire swing, which gave the girl the feeling of leaving earth each time she swung out above its slope. The branches above tangled into sunlight and blue sky and when Lucy swayed she didn't care if she ever came back down. She'd throw her head back and laugh and wait for the firm shove of her mother's hands that sent her flying once again.

This time of year had always been Lucy's favorite. Everybody just seemed happier, but the summer never lasted long. In a couple of months she'd be starting fourth grade. She was trying to make the most of her short time at home. Her mommy didn't play outside with her as much as she used to, but Lucy just assumed it was because she was turning nine soon and getting too old for some stuff. Used to on these days a family friend might pull into the driveway and drink a beer with her father. They'd grill out and cut up a watermelon. She'd smell the honeysuckle's sweet leaves before pinching the stem and dragging it through the bloom. Her father would wade into the creek below their yard for the smoothest stones to skip. The constant stream and wide-open sky were ingrained in her young heart.

Lucy peeled the scab from her leg and a bead of blood arose. She wiped the scab onto the porch step and with her palm smeared the blood into a streak down her leg. Her father stomped up the steps and looked down on her.

"Damn it, Lucy! You're too old to be making a mess of yourself like that! Get inside and clean that off!" John said. He tried not to curse at his daughter, but he'd been waiting on Sweetie Goodins all morning for a pill and wasn't feeling quite himself. He sat down on an old kitchen chair in front of the screen door and lit a cigarette. The Oldsmobile could wait until he was feeling better.

CHAPTER THREE

John and Anne Perley were two of the best young people Sweetie had known in his years pushing pills. When he pulled into their driveway that morning, he could see John sitting out on the front porch smoking a cigarette and tapping his foot like he always did when he hadn't got high yet. The younger man stood and leaned forward on the flimsy porch railing that was framed in with shabby two-by-fours and one-by-eight planks. Sweetie had helped him nail it all together when the young couple first had their daughter Lucy. They were just two kids themselves back then.

Sweetie's truck idled behind him as he got out and

stepped to the porch where John crushed his cigarette against the wooden railing.

"Howdy, howdy," Sweetie said as he started up the steps.

"How's it going, Sweet?"

"Keeping busy. Thought I'd come by before heading up to town. You and that little wife of yours want these last two I got?"

"I reckon so. God knows they're killing us but can't do much without them either." John stretched his neck out and spat into the yard, then scratched the back of his head. Sweetie rocked back on his heels, his hands stuffed into his pockets.

"I'll go in and get your money," John said. "You can come on in if you want. Anne's asleep, Lucy's somewhere playing."

"I need to get running here soon."

"I made some coffee."

"I've already had my coffee for the day. I need the money you owe me from the other day too. Tim is aiming to go to Lexington tomorrow to re-up and I'm broke."

The screen door clanged as John vanished inside and left Sweetie standing by himself. He turned to look back down the driveway, morning dew still shone on the grass. Sweetie thought about the little girl Lucy and how her day would be spent while her parents laid up high together. Couldn't be any worse for the poor girl than listening to them at each other's throats when they were dope sick. The door rattled behind Sweetie. He turned to see John holding out a handful of bills, crumpled ones and fives all half-heartedly folded together for this moment. Sweetie didn't even bother counting. He knew it didn't matter; he'd give them the pills no matter how much they had to offer. Their constant lies turned his stomach, but he just plain couldn't handle the begging. A grown man and woman with not an ounce of shame left in them. He gave in almost every time if he had anything on him. There were months when he winded up paying Tim back out of his own pocket.

"Let us know when you get some more, I'll get paid this Friday up at the mill."

"Why don't you ever just buy them from Tim himself?"

"He don't like to talk dope at work no more. Old boy last week asked him for something to make the day easier, fired him on the spot. Tim told him pack his shit up and get. Wouldn't even give him a ride back down to the main road from where we were logging." John spoke plainly like he didn't care one way or another. "You always done right by us anyways. Tim's a snake."

Sweetie stood for a time like he was thinking about what John had just told him, but it didn't surprise him any. Tim was paranoid, there wasn't any doubt about it.

"Here." Sweetie reached into his shirt pocket and took out a sandwich bag that looked oddly oversized to only hold two small tablets. John took the bag and straightened it out so he could see the little round, green pills nestled inside.

"She'll want to do both these the minute she wakes up. Like I said, give me a call when you're good again. I'll have more cash this weekend."

The first thing Sweetie did when he got back in his truck

was check the gas gauge, he figured he had enough to make it down to Tim's and back. As he drove, he couldn't help but rack his brain thinking of what all needed to be done back home. His father would spend the morning shuffling around the kitchen. The old man would probably make an egg for himself and then head outside to the porch to whittle the day away. Sweetie planned to help him weed out the garden once the day cooled off some.

Sweetie pulled up to the first red light in town, rolling his window down to breathe the morning air. He always enjoyed driving through town early before hardly anybody was out stirring. Mostly it was just him and the morning commuters. People getting gas and buying coffee at the Shell Mart before the long haul to another county where factory work had blossomed, somewhere they could earn a wage that made it worth the drive. It bothered Sweetie thinking about the couple from the corner store the day before. He prided himself on keeping his dealings private. Private as a fellow could in his line of work at least. Two strangers calling him out like that in the middle of broad daylight felt like a punch in the gut. He was thankful there hadn't been anybody else around, but it was just luck. That could happen anywhere he went, and he knew it. If he ever got busted by some nosy crew cut with a badge, it wouldn't take the state of Kentucky no time to lock his father away in a nursing home. He was starting to wonder if it was worth the risk—they mostly paid for what they needed off their social security even if it wasn't much. All it took was two loudmouths at the gas station and his world could come crashing down.

Case had probably been running his mouth to his little buddies up in town. That's what he kept telling himself. But really, he knew he'd been doing this long enough that plenty of folk knew him for what he was.

The light turned green and he put his foot to the gas thinking about the Perley family. He thought about John tapping his foot on his porch and Lucy always watching and listening somewhere nearby. He thought about how the boy Case Estes had looked sitting out at the corner stop. Two fine young men if they'd put their minds to anything worthwhile. Boys once full of life and willing to work hard, just plain good kids now destroyed by something no bigger than the tip of a pinky finger. Now neither of them was hardly worth a dime if they weren't expecting something from somebody in return.

Easing his foot off the gas pedal, the truck engine fluttered as he rolled by the courthouse and the police department. Sweetie and Tim had made runs to Lexington and some pharmacies down south for years, but he still got butterflies in his stomach every month they planned a pickup. Part of him always dreaded seeing Tim. Sweetie was the man's elder by a decade or more, but Tim was one of those men who reeked of a certain arrogance. The extra money was useful though, and it certainly kept him busy. His father's doctor bills kept pouring in through the mail. At the old man's last appointment, they had mentioned putting him in a facility. Sweetie wouldn't hear of it. But deep down he knew his own good health wouldn't keep forever, and the days he was able to care for both of them were almost up. For now, he was just worried about socking away enough cash to pay the bills and keep the house standing. Tomorrow's problems would be there when their time came.

Tim's house sat nestled towards the back of Stony Crossing, one of Turkeyfoot's few suburbs, full of brick houses with striped lawns and carefully trimmed hedges. Sweetie figured that Tim's mill had probably sold the builders most of the lumber when the neighborhood was first going up. Tim Stevens might have been a pill pusher, but he also ran a logging outfit. It was a small company, but they did a fair share of business in the state. That was how Tim got into the dope business to begin with. Not only did he hire some fellas with habits and histories, but some of his more straight and narrow guys got hurt on the job. When they couldn't work to pay the bills, all they had left was a hefty subscription of painkillers. It was a natural solution to their money problems, most of them didn't want to fool with pills anyway. And for Tim, it was a profit margin he couldn't stand to ignore. Once he knew how much money there was to be had selling pills, Sweetie came into the picture. Tim still had a company to run and a public appearance to maintain. Sweetie had more liberty in that regard. He could move freely during the day and to most curious onlookers he was just another old face in the community out piddling around.

It wasn't a bad deal for Sweetie even if he did take most of the risk. He didn't have the kind of cash to put up front like Tim did. They would head to Lexington and come back with a whole bag full of pharmacy-grade painkillers and muscle relaxers. He'd piece it out through the month to the folks he knew and visit Tim for more if needed.

The subdivision had a massive stone sign marking the entrance that simply read STONY CROSSING. It felt like a world apart from his own each time Sweetie drove up to it. Driveways were lined with new Acura SUVs and convertibles with more horsepower than he figured the owner could even handle. Sweetie never pulled into Tim's driveway, he just parked his truck at the curb and walked around to the backyard.

Tim's head was shaved clean and singed with a splash of cologne, a bronze bottle of something Sweetie imagined the man's wife had bought from Macy's in Lexington. His chest was burned red by the sun as he lay flat on his back with his arms splayed out. The wooden deck was stained cherry red, and Tim's legs stuck to the fat rubber bands that made up his lounge chair. On a glass table next to him sat a flip phone, a water bottle, a legal pad with a pen on top. Across his chest his Bible rested with its spine to the sky. Sweetie stood at the edge of the pool deck with his hands in his pockets.

"What do you know, man?" Sweetie said.

"What do any of us know, Sweetie?"

"Nothing any count for anything. Bit early to be out taking it easy by the pool, ain't it?"

"You're a wise man, Mr. Goodins."

"I'm a fool the same as you."

"No, my friend. You are a unique soul. You ever heard of Socrates? The philosopher?"

"I know he's dead. And that's about as far as my

knowledge of the ancient Greeks goes. I'd wager to say I'm not as well read as yourself," Sweetie said. Where he stood Sweetie could see across several of the neighboring backyards, all of them with their own pool and grill like they came standard with each new build.

"I reckon that's enough for most of us. But I know you didn't come over this morning to talk philosophy."

"No, I reckon there's business to tend to. I'm pretty much out. You got any more put back?"

"Sadly, no. That wife of mine has taken a liking to them herself, she took the bottles I kept. Migraines, she says. I think she just likes laying around in Lalaland all day."

"Well..." Sweetie swallowed and thought about what to say next. He knew once someone got a feel for it there wasn't much chance of turning back. It would only get worse from here. Sweetie could tell that Tim knew the same and changed the topic.

"When are we going to head back out on the road then?" Sweetie asked.

"What are you doing tomorrow? I got a deal lined up with those cutthroats in Lexington again."

"I just got a few things to take care of at the house. When you wanting to head up there?"

"I was thinking we'd leave early. Get up there about noon, that way we can get home before evening. Give you some time to take care of whatever you need to while there's still some daylight burning."

"I'll be over in the morning then. John's already telling me to give him a call when we get back."

"Perley?"

"Yeah, he works for you up at the sawmill."

"I never took him for a pillhead."

"They're mostly good kids, they just got a bad habit."

"You pray much, Mr. Goodins?"

"Not since my mother died. She always made one of us boys say grace before supper." Sweetie avoided eye contact with the sprawled-out man still kicking back in the lounge chair. Too comfortable in his sun-scorched flesh for Sweetie to understand.

"Never hurts for men in our line of work to get to know the Lord." Tim sat up to face Sweetie, he took his sunglasses off and squinted his eyes against the morning sun as it started to rise further above the distant treetops. Water dripped from his thighs to the burnished planks. "Christ said, 'Foxes have holes and birds of the air have nests, but the Son of Man has nowhere to lay his head.' It's always good to remember we're only passing through this world, Sweetie. Don't get too caught up in it. Lord knows I try not to."

Tim stood and dove into the deep end of the in-ground pool. Sunrays shimmered against the clear blue water. When the man came up at the other end, droplets of water cascaded from the top of his bald crown.

CHAPTER FOUR

As the evening faded Sweetie and his father rested against the bank of a hill that ran up from their field into brush and briar. They'd been weeding their small patch of tomatoes and peppers, which meant mostly Sweetie had been weeding while his father pointed out the places he'd missed and occasionally commented on the old days and how much sweat they'd poured into this soil. The older Goodins man insisted on putting his own crop down this season. It was a small patch, just six short rows that seemed to warp space and stretch out before your eyes.

It wasn't too hot out now that the sun was setting, but Sweetie had never been one for farmwork. He wiped at his neck with a handkerchief. His father twisted a plug of chewing tobacco up and plopped it in his jaw. Mostly neither of them spoke, but this was what Sweetie had always known. Few words passed between them even now as his father's time on earth was undoubtedly coming to its end. The sun crept down behind the mountains before them and sent dying swaths of sunburst pooling into the night sky where stars had begun to wink. Sweetie's mother had been dead for a few years now, and his father had grown hardheaded in his ways. Denser than normal that is. Nowadays hardly nothing store-bought was suitable. If he drank or cooked with water, it had to come from the spring up the mountain a ways. His father lined gallon jugs of the spring water along the base of the house, replacing a full jug with an empty when he used one up. When they were all gone, Sweetie and him would load them in the bed of the truck and drive up the hill to fill them again.

"I'm going to bed. I got to head up to Lexington with Tim tomorrow morning."

"Messing with them pillheads is going to get you killed."

"They ain't got one over on me yet," Sweetie said.

"You think I don't see the way they watch every time they come by looking for you? Acting all shifty like jackals. Worse off than jackals, they got the notions of man. They're liable to cave both of our heads in before it's all said and done."

"You need me to get you any groceries or anything while I'm out tomorrow? Fill your scripts?" His father didn't say anything right away. Sweetie palmed the grass and raised himself to his feet.

"I just need me some fresh water whenever you get back around this way. We'll go tomorrow evening once that sun ball decides to set down some."

Sweetie knew his father was right in what he said. One of them boys could get him down if they wanted to. They could take him for what little he had if they got desperate enough.

CHAPTER FIVE

Sweetie couldn't help but think about what his father had said as he pulled on his boots the next morning. *Jackals.* He knew they'd take anything they could get their hands on if he gave them a chance, but part of him felt obliged to them. He knew he was partially responsible for their state of being. But if it wasn't him, they'd find someone else to buy the stuff off of, not that that excused his role in the whole mess. He couldn't help but keep running back and forth peddling to them, he didn't know what else he'd be doing besides sitting up with the old man all day. He'd go insane.

Sweetie drove from his house, toward the top of the mountain, to town and back again at least five, maybe six, times a day. Sometimes he'd even make a few trips into the next county over. If it was the first of the month, when a lot of people drew their check, he'd tell some folk to meet him up at the Save-A-Lot parking lot. But him and Tim were behind this month on their usual pickup, so his routine was a bit off its rhythm. He had told John he'd let him know when they got back, but already this morning his cell phone had about rang out of his pocket.

"You got any of those?"

"Say, you have any Oxy on you?"

"You got a few of those Perc thirties?"

The same questions from every pillhead he knew, and not a one of them would leave him be until they got theirs.

"No, damn it! I told you yesterday I got to head up there today," he snapped at John while driving through town.

"Let me know when y'all are heading on back this way." John had been falling into a rut the same as they all did. Couldn't get the buzz he had grown accustomed to, so he bought more and took more. John had his head on a bit straighter than most of Sweetie's buddies. Having a wife and daughter that relied mostly on him kept him in check. His wife Anne was hooked on the things too, but the two at least kept a roof over the kid's head. John's mom was known to help them out when they blew all their money getting high. They were always Sweetie's first stop when he got back from dealing with Tim. The Perleys would buy a good bag full to hold them over for at least a few days.

When Sweetie knocked at Tim's front door the morning's fog was still lifting. Tim answered wearing a white bathrobe with coffee stains down the left-hand side. He held a white mug in one hand and his Bible flipped open in the other.

"Care to take your boots off? Just had new wood flooring put in. Say, count that money on the table and double-check I ain't shorting nobody. Last thing we need is to get ourselves dumped in a shallow hole somewhere." Tim walked away as Sweetie closed the door behind him.

"Sweetie, the book of Judges ends saying, 'In those days there was no king in Israel; everyone did what was right in his own eyes.' Where do you reckon that puts a man who does wrong even in his own eyes?"

"No place good, I'm sure." Sweetie sat on the couch; his socks slippery on the new hardwood. He felt like a child with his boots off.

"We worship a living, supernatural God, Sweetie. One of infinite force and grace. A King of the Universe, Christ on the cross, His blood for our sin. A violent death, but also a rebirth to set the cosmos flush. He's the Alpha and the Omega."

"How can you do what we do and still believe in all that?" Sweetie asked.

"How could I do what we do and not believe in all this?" Tim said.

Tim gulped down the rest of his coffee and scribbled something in his notepad. Sweetie started counting out twenty- and hundred-dollar bills into neat stacks on a marble coffee table that sat in the middle of the room.

After a couple of hours on the interstate they finally made it to Lexington. They took Tim's new truck, but Sweetie drove. The interstate exit curved in a wide J until it came back around to face a series of apartment complexes. Gas stations and fast-food restaurants lined the busy four-lane bypass going in both directions. The parking lot they pulled into was full of rows of vehicles, and two gray buildings stood like a pair of obelisks blocking out the skyline on either side.

Sweetie cut Tim's truck into the parking lot and wedged the F-150's wide front end between a rusted-out Toyota and a dinged-up minivan. Tim sat in the passenger seat with his sunglasses on and a bottle of water between his knees. He cursed to himself and punched buttons on his cell phone.

"Bastard never responds when I get up here. I've never in my life had to beg someone to take a bag of hundred-dollar bills off me like I do this piece of work. Wait till you see these guys, they're some real pricks. From way down south or some shit, if you know what I mean."

Sweetie kept glancing in the rearview mirror, trying to scan the parking lot. Tim sucked down the rest of his water bottle and pitched the empty plastic shell into the back seat. A bell sounded from the phone and Tim stopped squirming.

"I want you to come in here with me. They tried to get funny on me last time we came up." Tim pulled a ziplock bulging with money from under his seat. Sweetie cut the engine and thought again about his father's warning. If the boys back home would kill him for some money and dope, some strangers in a city apartment wouldn't think twice about slitting his throat.

"What do you mean they were acting funny?"

"They tried to give me some fake shit. Synthetic stuff. Looks just like the real pills."

"What's the difference?"

"It was cheaper, but I don't buy anything I don't understand. This time I'm asking for some though. We'll see what people think. If we can sell it for the same as an Oxy or more and pay less on our end, then I'm in business."

"Probably that shit they bring over the border. Fentanyl. I seen it on the news. Supposed to be deadly stuff," Sweetie said. He didn't have no qualm against making more money, but he knew people like the Perleys would kill themselves if they got ahold of that stuff. Tim shoved the bag of money down the front of his pants, and they took off walking across the parking lot. Sweetie's heart thumped as they approached the lobby door of the apartment. Tim buzzed a plastic box mounted to the brick wall, but nobody answered it. In the bottom of Sweetie's heart, he hoped this would be it. Maybe their Mexican friends had got busted or got tired of fooling with two hicks. He could just go home and help his dad fill his water jugs.

Clack. The glass door sounded. Tim pulled it open, and they quickly stepped through the lobby into a stairwell off the side. It was half lit with weak lightbulbs hanged sporadically. Sweetie lost count of how many flights they climbed, but it had to be more than three. He was glad he'd stayed active walking the hills in his older age. Tim barely broke a sweat. The man still had his sunglasses on and kept glancing at the cell phone. He looked more like someone on vacation than someone trafficking narcotics as they finally pushed into a hallway. The walls were bare cinder block, and the doors were made of metal. It had been a long time since Sweetie had seen the inside of county lockup, but that's what came to mind as he followed Tim to the end of the corridor.

Tim knocked the way a neighbor might when dropping by, and they were quickly welcomed in by a Hispanic man with hair buzzed short and letters tattooed across his face. Inside the apartment was mostly bare; Sweetie could tell it was merely a place for conducting business. They stepped into a dim living room thick with smoke, the sound of music thumping. Sweetie knew the noon sun was bright outside, but the windows had been taped off with cardboard and aluminum foil.

"My hillbilly friends! I'm so glad to see you."

"Turn that shit off," Tim said, waving his hands in front of his face. Sweetie peered down the hallway, but could only see darkened doorways and more barren walls.

"What you want this time?" the man with the tattoos asked.

"I want my usual, but I want some of that synthetic too. You still got it?"

"Got it? That's mostly what we deal in now, hillbilly. Easier to get, more money in our pocket, you understand."

"I'm no dumbass, I do understand. That's why I'm asking for it. I want to see how people like it before I buy too much though." Tim sat down on the couch and kicked his boots up on the table.

"Hey, hey, hey! No boots on the table, how many times I have to tell you that? Were you raised in a barn?" The man lit a cigarette and vanished down the hallway into one of the darkened rooms. It bothered Sweetie that he hadn't thought to watch which room exactly, but he was distracted by Tim's behavior. His heart was pounding in his chest and Tim was bantering back and forth like this was an old friend. Sweetie usually just waited outside— he never imagined the two cutting up like this while a deal went down. He was ready to leave. He looked up to realize the ink-faced man was carrying two fat ziplock bags of pills back into the room.

"You tell me, which is fake and which is real?" he said, tossing them onto the table at Tim's feet.

"Shit, he fools with them more than me. What you say, Mr. Goodins?" Tim nodded towards Sweetie. Sweetie picked each bag up and turned them over. As far as he could tell each was filled with Oxycodone and Percocet, some stamped to mark a thirty milligram and others with a fifteen or a ten. Sweetie couldn't tell a difference and he knew Case or John or anybody he fooled with couldn't either and wouldn't care to nohow.

"So how much you want?" the man asked, seeing that Sweetie couldn't tell. Tim stretched out on the couch and unlatched his belt so that he could pull the bag of money out of his pants. Once he had himself situated again, he carefully counted out several rolls of bills onto the table.

"There's for my usual. Now how much for that synthetic?"

"That would be about two more bands."

"What's a band? You're gonna need to speak English, I'm getting old."

"Two Gs, hillbilly. Two thousand."

"Shit," Tim said. "Alright, just give it to me. Somebody'll buy it, won't they, Sweetie?" Tim laughed as he tossed another fistful of bills into the pile.

CHAPTER SIX

It all only took about thirty minutes, but it might as well have been hours to Sweetie. Back outside in the dense parking lot, Tim flung open the truck door, hopped right back up into his seat, and tossed his two new ziplock bags into the center console.

On the drive back down, Sweetie took the interstate as far as he could, then they stopped off to fill Tim's truck up with gas. Tim was always bold on these trips. Sweetie figured he liked getting out of his little suburbia paradise when he could. He felt bulletproof out on their runs. Didn't make no difference if twenty-thousand-dollars' worth of dope rested between them. Sweetie knew Tim would come back out of the gas station with a six-pack of cold beer and crack one open for the rest of the ride home. A little ritual to reward himself. It always made Sweetie nervous. As he topped the gas off and screwed the cap back on, Tim came strutting across the parking lot cradling a brown sack in one hand and balancing two sandwiches wrapped in white paper in his other.

"Hope you like bologna and 'maters, 'cause that's what I got you." Tim swung himself up into the crew cab. "What do you think of these fake pills?"

"Well, they'll probably sell quick. He's right about that."

"But?"

"I can't say I want much to do with them. I'd hate to get wrapped up in someone dying."

"They'd have to catch you red-handed just about to trace it back to us," Tim said.

"It just don't sit right with me. Pills is one thing, but this stuff is more like poison it seems." Sweetie could tell Tim had been banking on him to move most of the fentanyl for him, and the man's gears were turning to work out another option.

"What do you think of that John Perley boy? He seems like a pretty hard worker up at the sawmill," Tim said.

Sweetie bumped the key and the shiny new Ford erupted to life immediately. He was caught off guard by Tim mentioning John's name.

"Like I said before, he's an alright feller. Just let himself get hooked on dope." Sweetie shifted the truck down into drive and glanced in the rearview mirror. "He'll work when he's got to. We've poured concrete here and there together. Other than the old man, he's the closest I got to family; I've known that boy for a long time now."

"You think I can trust him?" Tim asked. Sweetie wondered why the interest in John when earlier it seemed as though the two hardly spoke at work.

"I think you can trust him. As long as you ain't between him and a pill."

"I think I can manage as much as that."

Sweetie was glad to be putting the city and larger towns behind them. The farther away they got from the interstate the better he felt. He settled into the black leather seat and loosened up as he turned onto familiar roads near home. They passed fields of wildflowers and weeds that crept alongside the highway where the county maintenance crew had neglected their route. Thin shoots of lavender and goldenrod swayed in the summer air. Tim rolled down the passenger window and pitched an empty beer can out. Without missing a beat, he had another can out of its thin plastic ring and popped the tab, foamy suds spilling down the man's hand. Sweetie watched the empty bounce across the pavement in the side-view mirror. They rode in silence awhile and soon Sweetie could see Turkeyfoot Mountain rising up in the distance.

CHAPTER SEVEN

That same evening Sweetie and his father loaded up the back of his truck with the empty milk jugs just as he'd promised. Towards the top of the mountain the tangled road widened out, and Sweetie parked on the shoulder. Each trip he told his father the same thing.

"You just sit here, and I'll fill them up real quick."

Each trip the old-timer spat back, "I reckon surely I got one more in me."

His father shuffled from the bed of the truck to a spring coming off the mountain. He carried a gallon jug in each hand. The plastic was stained from hundreds of trips to the spring.

Sweetie stared down the ditch line. The shallow passage

was clogged with paper bags and Mountain Dew bottles, crumpled cigarette packs and the occasional dope needle.

The spring water trickled down a small face of slate rock. The jugs filled slowly, so slowly that Sweetie wondered if there was enough water rolling off the mountain to fill them or if it was aiming to run dry right there and then.

He could buy his father enough water to last a year for what it cost in gas to drive out to the spring, but the man wouldn't hear of it. Sweetie couldn't think of a time that his father ever looked so weak. The old man made his way back to the truck with a gallon straining each wrist, his joints crackling beneath his flesh.

A car full of drunks whizzed by. A little souped-up Pontiac with baby moon tires that shone in the evening light as they rolled around the curve. The woman in the passenger seat cackled gladly, her lungs full of the laughter that comes with anticipation of another night running wild. They came and went in a tear, and then the road was silent again. The old Goodins man heaved the jugs of water into the truck bed and whispered a curse. He favored one knee for a moment then eased his shrunken frame onto the bumper to rest. He breathed in the thin evening air and spoke without looking at Sweetie.

"I need some new jugs."

"What you need is some new knees." Sweetie spat into the ditch after he spoke.

His father had already snatched two more plastic jugs and headed back to the spring. Sweetie watched the old man's loafers slowly shuffle, knees and hands shivering as though the littered ground beneath the two men trembled. His steps halted as he made his way up to where the stream dribbled down. He searched for footing that wasn't there. His left leg straightened out as his loafer lost traction in the mud. He plopped down on his tail end with a squish.

He didn't try to get up right away and Sweetie didn't move to help him. The spring water pattered at his father's feet that pointed to the sky in front of him like a child's. Sweetie's chest swelled with a foolish anger at the stream. The old man's bald head slumped between his shoulders.

Sweetie made his way towards his father still planted on his bottom in the mud. The front of his overalls was a deeper blue as more water splashed onto his chest. His wrinkled white knuckles squeezed onto the plastic jugs' handles.

Sweetie hooked his father's elbow and pulled him to his feet with ease. Still shaken from the fall, he stood and found his footing, too stubborn to turn loose of his grip on the empty jugs.

"Give me that," Sweetie said and snatched one of the jugs. The old man grabbed onto his son's shoulder to steady himself.

"Might as well get these last two," he said

He plunged one of his loafers into the murky puddle beneath the stream then held a jug up to the trickle. He struggled to hold it steady. The more water that filled it the more his hands tremored. The water lapped at the mouth of the plastic container and spilled out over his wrinkled skin. Sweetie expected him to drop it, but he pulled it back to his chest and screwed the cap on.

"Maybe we ought to head over to that Walmart for water next month," the old man said. For the first time in his life, Sweetie could hear quit in his father's voice as the old man turned back to the truck. Sweetie filled the last jug on his own.

CHAPTER EIGHT

Sweetie Goodins dreamed of gaped mouths with soft pink gums, begging him for mercies. His hands and forearms dripped with blood as he fed them.

Each morning when he awoke, he listened to hear his father shuffling around in the kitchen making coffee, stoking the furnace, letting the front door clang shut on his way outside to tamp down a fresh pipeful of tobacco. The house was silent. As the old man had aged, he had begun sleeping later some mornings. Sweetie had the shade pulled tight, but it was still dark out as far as he could tell.

Sweetie's mind noticed an unfamiliar banging, like metal and wood clobbering against one another. He sighed and pulled himself up from the mattress to make his way down the hall. Walking out onto the front porch he found an old van parked in the driveway with nobody in it. Sweetie stepped down and rounded the corner to his yard where he spotted Case at his shed. The padlock and chain that once secured the rickety door now lay busted up in a pile on the ground alongside a large new sledgehammer with a bright neon handle and a shining silver head. Case sat crisscross in the doorway of the shed with a gas can next to him, sucking on the end of a rubber hose, the other end dipped into Sweetie's lawn mower.

"Have you completely lost your mind?" Sweetie asked, standing in his night drawers and a plain white undershirt.

"I just needed some gas to get uptown, Sweetness. I didn't want to disturb you over something silly like lawn-mower gas. You know me and James are good for it."

"I know no such thing. And don't start with the Sweetness shit this morning. I know you're high as a kite already."

"Shit, I wish I was."

"I swear to you, boy, I will shoot you dead where you sit if you don't get in that junky van and get down that driveway."

Case finally got the gas flowing from the lawn mower into his empty can. He spat and then wiped his mouth on the tail end of his shirt as a soft pitter-patter sounded and sped up to a trickle.

"I'm going, I'm going. Say, you like that sledgehammer there? Brand-new. It's got that rubberized grip on the handle and everything. Look at how clean the head on that sucker is, you could eat off it. I'd be willing to get in a hot swap for it—you got any of those little green fifteens?"

"How about I just keep it for the gas and my busted shed door?"

"Well, I reckon if that'll suit you."

Sweetie eyed the tool and snatched it up. He swung it over his shoulder and started back towards the house to make some coffee.

By the time the sun had risen Sweetie was sitting in the Perleys' living room. John had been crawling the walls again. Lucy screamed and cried from her bedroom down the hallway. Mamaw Perley had given her money to spend at the Dollar General, but her mother and father weren't in any mood to take her uptown. Anne sat at the kitchen table tapping cigarette ash into a coffee mug. The woman stared into the mouth of the cup blankly. Sweetie and John sat on opposite ends of the couch while the older man counted out Percocet on the coffee table. He gently slid them down to John one at a time with the tip of his index finger, like a cashier figuring a customer's change.

"Fuck, man, I thought you was gonna call us last night. I just kept waiting for my phone to ring," John said.

"I had to help the old man at the house."

"You hear they locked James Estes up again?" John said, his arms crossed tightly to his chest.

"Good. Oughta sober him up. Both them boys are

trouble. I just talked to his brother this morning." Sweetie Goodins didn't take his eyes from the cluster of pills.

John squirmed in his corner of the couch watching the old man count. His guts pinched up inside of him and a tickle settled deep in his throat. His sweating stopped just knowing that he could soon use. Lucy's cries died down briefly but came back hoarse to demand attention. The girl's ragged screams sounded like they caught and tore in her throat before echoing into the living room.

"Will you go back there and shut her up?" John glared across the room into the kitchen where Anne still sat in her own little world. Someplace she went that crumbled his ego like soggy drywall, dreams of a home in the suburbs with hardwood floors and a paved driveway lined with flowers. A place John could never give her. The shortcoming settled over the man in a sheet of hot contempt whether it was imagined or not.

Anne's eyes rolled up from the coffee cup and crossed the room to where her husband sat. Her glazed-over stare seemed to clear briefly. Lucy had been Anne's anchor. But there were nights when she had wished on stars and prayed to gods foreign from her own that the little brown-haired girl would not be there to weigh her back down to earth. When she was high, it was at least a break. A break from the whining and a break from the cooking and a break from the *Mommy, Mommy, Mommy*.

"Give me a minute." Anne's words spilt from her mouth. The woman's eyelids sagged down over her heavy brown eyes and her head lulled back down towards the coffee cup where her cigarette had almost burned down to its filter. She pinched the butt and mashed it between her thumb and forefinger, mangling the stained cotton filter and dropping it into the cup with the ash. The woman tucked her chin against her chest and her arms fell to hang limply at her sides.

John shook his head and sat forward on the couch. Lucy's cries tapered off as Sweetie counted out the last of the pills.

"There. We ought to be square for now at least," Sweetie said. He silently rolled up his pant leg and tucked the plastic bag of pills deep into his cowboy boot before standing, straightening his jeans, and pulling the front door closed behind him on his way out.

John scooped his pills into his hands, dropping all of them except for one into a baggy of his own. Anne was still slumped over at the kitchen table. He twisted the top of the bag off and tossed it back to the center of the coffee table before walking to the back room and looking in on Lucy, who had finally cried herself to sleep. The girl's face was round and soft, her tears had left streaks of red down her cheeks. Her chest rose only to fall again, smooth as seasons come and gone.

CHAPTER NINE

For the next couple of months John had stayed on a regular schedule with Tim Stevens' logging outfit. The sawmill Tim's crew ran was one of the best money could buy. John knew Mr. Stevens had been doing well on this most recent plat, but he hadn't known how well exactly. The acreage had a lot of good timber and they had just about locked down the market, at least most of it around Turkeyfoot. There was still other lumber moving in and out of Kentucky, mostly corporate wood getting shipped. Tim's was all local, and the snotty folk building their retirement cabins in the neighboring counties loved that aspect. They didn't see the side of *local* that John knew.

The old-timers had already spent a good half hour

looking over the new addition to the jobsite this morning. They chewed tobacco and circled the machine. The blade and its polished teeth were shielded by neon orange sheet metal plastered with large, clear safety warnings.

He couldn't care less about the fancy new sawmill. All it meant to him was the boss was making even more than it seemed and it made his daily pay seem that much more pitiful. On that foggy morning, he sat back on a stump while the others gawked at the piece of machinery like it was an idol with a higher power.

Before long Tim's big new Ford came crawling up the steep gravel road. Looking time was over now. John hopped up from his stump and headed towards the rusty work truck that hauled all of them up together. He reached behind the seat and pulled out a thick pair of leather gloves that fit snug over his bony hands. He never acted like he knew Mr. Stevens when they were sawing lumber, even though he'd been around him some doing business with Sweetie. He was surprised Tim had even let him come work for him. Then again, he was just the type Tim wanted working for him, the kind he could control and keep happy with the promise of a pill at the end of a hard day. He hated Tim for that.

He thought about walking on down the hill and back towards town. Somebody would let him hitch a ride there or up to Sweetie's. Somebody would be sure to have a little medicine for him this morning. His hips felt tight, and the day hadn't even started yet. He wondered why Case hadn't shown up. He'd probably done exactly what John was thinking on, said to hell with it and caught a buzz instead of working like a mule for a man who looked down his nose at you. He wanted to be home with Anne and Lucy, but they needed the money. They were behind on almost everything and he knew Sweetie had cut him a deal this week for the pills. If he didn't work, they'd be sick and wouldn't have lights to boot.

"Say, John." Tim's booming voice calling his name startled him.

"Yes, sir?"

"You know Mr. Goodins don't you?"

"My family's known his for quite a while."

"He'll be coming over to pour a slab of concrete at my house this weekend. Give him a call if you want to make some extra cash."

"I'll give him a holler. I ain't afraid of some extra work," John said.

Sweetie and John rode in silence on Saturday morning. The truck's headlights offered little guidance against the thick sheet of fog. Soon the Kentucky summer sun would rise and awaken the hills. By then the two men would be drenched in sweat and up to their ankles in cement.

Tools clattered in the bed of the truck as they rocked through the curves coming off the mountain. The bull float and hand trowels knocked against one another.

"You set me loose with one of those trowels and I'll have this slab so slick a fly would slip on it." John's bony jawline popped as he spoke. He was chatty and trying to make small talk, but Sweetie never responded to his brag. They pulled into the Stony Crossing subdivision and drove right up into Tim Stevens' backyard. They unloaded the tools and waited for the concrete truck to arrive.

Around noon they stopped working and ate a small lunch together. Their jeans were splotched with small clumps of drying cement, their backs and shoulders ached under the strain of pushing the wheelbarrow and raking. Back at Sweetie's truck they ate Little Debbie cakes and stared at their morning's work. The slab they'd poured was squared off against Tim's brick home and pool deck. Two-by-fours banked in the soft cement mixture as it hardened.

"How long you reckon it'll take to set up?" John asked.

"Same as every other damn job you've done with me. I'll come by in the morning to check it and get our money from Tim." Sweetie slapped shut the lid of his cooler and downed the rest of his soda pop before pitching the can into the bed of the truck.

"Tomorrow? That wasn't the deal. I need money today!" John backhanded his own can of pop off the tailgate of the truck. The sticky drink splattered on both of them before landing with a thud in the grass, suds foaming out of its mouth.

"Well, I want you to look. You need some dope that bad, you fucking cry baby? Go spray the bull float off before the cement dries to it," Sweetie said. "There's a water hose at the front of the house. I'm going to try to smooth this last corner out some." Sweetie tossed the cooler into the back seat of the truck.

John sucked on the tail end of a cigarette. He gazed over the flat gray surface of concrete and tried to calm himself. He walked away mouthing petty curses at Sweetie but snatched up the bull float by its handle. He flipped his cigarette butt into the yard and plucked a bright green leaf from the tree above the patio. It was wide and light in the palm of his hand, its flesh softer than his own. He crumpled it in his fist.

"You think he'd care if I went into the bathroom?" John asked.

"Just wait, damn it. Don't bother them none."

"I ain't playing man, I gotta shit! There ain't no waiting, I can either do it inside or squat over there by his precious box trimmed hedges."

"Will you shut up? Will you shut up for five minutes?" Sweetie said. He rose to face John but was still down on his knees with a trowel in hand. Sweat dripped from his head and gray cement was smeared up the length of his forearms. Some of the mixture was streaked across his face from wiping at his brow.

"You go on in there and do what you need to do. But I'll tell you another thing: so much as a pop can goes missing in there and I'm telling the man exactly the rogue who took it was," Sweetie said.

"Goddamn! Here we go with this shit, us friends and all and you still make me out to be a thief. Right in front of the Lord above. I don't give a fuck about Tim Stevens' pop or whatever else he has in there!"

"Just take your boots off when you go inside. He just had that flooring put down."

John let himself in through the garage door that Tim had left open for them in case they needed any of his tools. When John stepped into the kitchen it felt like the life his wife always dreamed of. The kitchen was blindingly white, the cabinets and drawers had shining golden knobs and handles everywhere he looked. There wasn't a doubt in his heart that the countertops were real marble, and directly in the center of the large kitchen area was an island. The heavy square was topped with a cutting block. A piece of red meat and a silver knife lay alone under the light above. John looked around for a hallway, but before he stepped through the kitchen Tim turned the corner.

"John Perley, good to see you, buddy. It's looking good out there. Y'all need any drinks?"

"We got it pretty much licked. I was just looking for the bathroom if y'all don't mind."

"Oh sure, it's right down the hall here." Tim motioned to where he had just come from. "Hey, before you go, I got something I want you to try out for me. Follow me back here."

They walked to a darkened guest bedroom near the back of the house. Inside there was a perfectly made bed with a plush comforter that looked like no one had ever even slept under it. Suits and dresses were piled neatly on top of a recliner in the corner of the room, each zipped up in a plastic covering. Tim got down on all fours and reached under the frame of the bed.

"Damn it, I always shove this thing so far back I can't hardly get a grip on it." The man struggled for a moment and grunted. A black firebox slid out onto the carpet between them. Without standing up Tim took his keys from his pocket and flipped the top open.

"Now I want you to be careful with this stuff. But I want to know what you think. And be generous now, get some others' opinions as well if you can. If you can sell that whole bag, I got some more stashed too," Tim said, holding a yellow envelope up to John.

"What is this?"

"Give it a look when you get home. It's fentanyl, a synthetic opioid. Mr. Goodins doesn't want to fool with it, so I'm in a bind. You could really help me out here."

"I'll see what I can do. I might know some boys," John said as he folded the envelope and tucked it safely down his pocket. Tim locked the box up again and showed John out to the bathroom across the hall.

CHAPTER TEN

Broken white clouds stretched out across the sky, glistening in the sun like tiny, sharp teeth. Anne Perley found herself wishing they'd gnash away and tear open the heavens so that a billowing crash of rain might pour down and fill the valleys flush to the mountaintops. She pulled a pair of wide sunglasses down over her eyes and snapped her fingers at Lucy.

"Hurry up, girl! I'm fixin' to leave you!"

Lucy came running from around the trailer with a small purse hanging around her neck, its plastic, glossy finish shining in the sunlight. She climbed up into the passenger seat of the Cutlass and settled into the crimson cloth seat next to her mother. Anne slammed the long heavy car door and gave the key a bump; the carburetor coughed, and Anne pumped the gas pedal, fluttering the engine into a roar.

In town Anne pulled the Cutlass up in front of a redbrick building. A corner of the building laid in a crumpled heap, but the foundation stood strong. There were no signs on the structure other than a series of three gold numbers plated across a heavy black door.

"I'll be right back, honey," Anne said. She gave Lucy a pat on the thigh, grabbed her purse, and slammed the car door shut.

A stiff breeze passed through the Oldsmobile's windows. The summer sun baked the car's flaking off-white paint. Rap music thumped from the other side of the redbrick wall, and Lucy's hair stuck to her forehead with sweat. The girl stared across the street where a man slept on the curb. His camo cargo pants were split at the shins, and his cheeks looked like shallow pits in his face.

Some days they spent all morning at the building. If they were still there in the afternoon, her mom would rush trying to make it back home before her daddy did.

The black door swung open and closed again, Anne climbed into the driver seat and glanced at herself in the rearview mirror before shifting the car into gear. Cross-eyed and numb, she wheeled the long nose of the Oldsmobile out on the main drag towards Walmart.

All summer long she had spent days like this with her mother. Before doing any shopping, they always stopped in the restroom. Lucy counted the bathroom tiles off in her head. Her eyes followed the black and white patterns down to the corner of the room before darting across to the other side. Anne dug through her purse between her ankles for her pocket mirror to crush a pill up. Lucy always thought her mommy's purse smelled like cotton balls and candy. Crumpled receipts and loose tampons covered the top, but past them pennies and sticks of gum had sunk to the bottom lining to settle in. The side pockets held lip balm, and folded in her wallet were dollar bills she knew her mommy kept tucked away from her daddy. She watched as her mother pinched one nostril shut with an index finger and snorted the white powder off the smooth, shining surface.

"How about we get you a toy, Lucy girl?"

"I just want to go home," Lucy said, never looking from the tiles on the wall.

Back in the car, Lucy's bag felt warm in her lap, having sat in the car most of the morning with the sun burning overhead. The cloth seat was scratchy against the back of her knees, and she could smell the heat of the car, stale and heavy in her throat like smoke. Lucy knew when they got back home her mom would go straight to the bathroom and stay locked in there until it was almost time for her daddy to get off work.

CHAPTER ELEVEN

Back at home the toilet seat was cold against the bottom of Anne's thighs. The woman rested her eyes and leaned forward, cupping her chin in her palm, her elbows against her knees. She wiped at her nose. A crushed Percocet still tickled her nasal cavity; it felt like something dripping down the back of her throat. On the bathroom sink was an empty bottle of hand soap, a grimy toothbrush holder, and a blank saucer with a shortcut straw resting in its center.

Anne snapped her eyes open and reached for the saucer, but just grazed it with her fingertips. She fumbled for its edge as it fell to the bathroom floor, where it shattered into pieces large and small. Losing her balance, she slipped forward off the toilet seat onto her palms and knees. Shards of glass sliced deep into Anne's palms. Her hands seeped bright red over what was left of the small plate. She didn't even try to get up. Anne reclined between the toilet and the sink cupboard, perfectly content with her heart melting out of her chest to stain the rest of the linoleum-tiled floor while she dreamed of the past.

Her stomach bulged tight from the pressure of her baby girl inside. Lucy was due to come in December. Anne prayed at night that it wouldn't be snowing when her daughter came into this world. It had already been cold for a November. Anne straightened a wooden coffee table in front of their couch. It was a green couch, one that John bought from his drinking buddy. It was made of cloth with cigarette burns and strange stains.

    John would be home soon. He'd been pouring concrete with Sweetie all weekend long. It was hard work but paid well, and he had promised to buy Anne a new couch before the baby came. Fresh and firm, one you could sink right into and take a nap.

    Anne peeked at the clock on the wall and wiped the kitchen counter. She filled a glass of water and walked to the living room. She sat on the old couch with her water and began picking at the cigarette burns. The cheap fiber that held the cushion's guts together had turned black and brittle where the tip of a Marlboro or maybe a Pall Mall had fallen. Anne plucked at the fabric until she had loosened a piece from the cloth. She rolled it between her thumb and index finger and flicked it across the living room.

Outside the winter sun had started dropping down behind the hills. Anne laid down and wrapped her arms around her pregnant stomach. She was excited about having some company on days like today, even if it was a crying baby. She would be happy loving her daughter, waiting for her husband to come home splattered with concrete mix. She looked forward to bright summer days when the sun didn't dip behind the trees so early of the evening.

Hours passed and Anne still hadn't moved. She was curled up with her pants around her ankles, a heap on the bathroom floor. Not flat but crumpled like a sack of rotten potatoes. Dried blood was caked to her knees and palms. Her arms were bent stiff, backward against the crook of her elbow.

Lucy listened for her mother from the hallway. She sat by the door and waited for the handle to turn and her mother to come out as normal. She would be a little foggy, but she'd straighten herself up and cook spaghetti or Hamburger Helper or whatever they'd eat for dinner that night. Lucy cradled her knees and strained her ear against the thin wooden door, listening for anything to let her know her mother was still moving around inside.

You better come on, Mommy, he's gonna be home. The girl attempted to will her mother out, the warning she ached to utter trapped in her throat. Inside, Anne's ears were clogged with the sweet coo of painkillers. Lucy listened for a breath, the sound of the toilet flushing, the faucet running, but only heard silence.

Lucy knew it was too late. She'd heard the work crew's truck dropping her father off in the driveway. John was on his way up the porch steps. Lucy sat frozen on the hallway floor, pinching threads of shaggy carpet between her fingers.

"Anne? Lucy?" John called out walking into the empty living room. He turned the corner and his eyes fell upon his daughter in the hallway.

"What are you doing, honey?"

"Waiting on Mommy to get done in the bathroom."

"How long has she been in there for?" he asked.

"I don't know, awhile." The girl wouldn't look up, she tucked her legs up under her as her father stepped over to the doorway.

"Anne!" he shouted and listened for a response.

It felt like the most silent second of Lucy's life. Her father didn't say anything else. He took one firm kick and buckled the flimsy doorframe in on itself. The man's muddy boot print smeared across the wood. He pushed it the rest of the way through with his hands until it hung loosely from its hinges. John glared down at his wife lumped on the bathroom floor like a damp towel.

"What in the fuck are you doing?!" his broad throat strained.

Anne's eyes rolled back into their proper place and focused on her husband above. John grabbed a fistful of hair and drug her through the hallway to the living-room floor. He pulled her across the length of the room and pushed her face into the carpet. Anne's knees stung as they scratched against the rug.

"I'm out working my ass off and you can't even watch our daughter?"

He went into the kitchen, pulled a tin box out from under the sink, and flung it open on the countertop.

"You didn't get it from here, so where'd you go? Who'd you go fuck today for a hit?"

He took out their sack of pills and grabbed two for himself, grinding them up right there on the counter with the butt of his cigarette lighter.

"Where'd your mommy take you today, Lucy?" he hollered down the hall. Lucy cried and held herself tight and bit her bottom lip shut. Anne had made her way up from the floor. She pressed the heels of her palms against her eye sockets and raked her fingers through her hair.

"Just go on back to your room and play, honey. Don't pay no mind to him," Anne said to Lucy.

That night, Lucy watched from her bedroom window as clouds filled the evening sky and spilled out over the hills. Lightning cracked within the great rolling behemoths above. They'd glow momentarily before returning to dark shadows that reached back over the ridge, well into infinity as far as she could tell. Lucy laid silent in her bed while the rain showers beat down on the other side of the ceiling. Shadows glided across the beam of light that shone through the bottom of her door. Her parents' muffled screams rapped at her little heart from the living room. She finally mustered the courage to walk out, just in time to watch from the hallway as her mother snatched up her purse and car keys and marched out into the rainy night. A strange sounding engine revved up and the wheels scratched through gravel, screeching sharply when they hit pavement at the end of the driveway.

CHAPTER TWELVE

The next morning the sun came back out and made the day muggy. Patches of mud and standing rainwater filled the yard. Lucy floated just high enough to eyeball the rusty top of their trailer, her shirt rising above her belly button as her glistening brunette hair trailed in the sky and she plummeted back down towards the static black trampoline. Bright green stains spread across the vinyl siding of the Perleys' trailer. The splotches started dark in the center and faded away as they moved outwards. When she went out to play, her father lay snoring in the center of the living-room floor. The Cutlass was still parked at the top of the driveway. What was left of the broken bathroom door rested flat on the front lawn;

thick, unkempt grass caressed its brown edges, while fat drops of dew melted away in the harsh morning sun.

CHAPTER THIRTEEN

When Anne left home, she never went too far. Case Estes would usually have her if he was feeling lonely. The two of them pulled up to a pump at the Happy-Top Corner Stop in the Astro van. The gas station parking lot was bare under the noon sun, other than an empty picnic table by the storefront. The usual dusty potholes were flush with rainwater from the storm the night before. Case counted out single dollar bills onto the dash of his van while Anne dug through her purse for spare change.

Shallow white clouds floated by overhead. Glancing up at them always made Anne feel like a fish at the bottom of the river watching the surface shimmer above. She was surprised that she had never seen broken twigs or the occasional piece of garbage floating by in the skyline. She pinched her bone-thin thighs while Case tried to time the pump so that it stopped exactly at $2.63. The numbers ticked up on a gallon counter from a previous decade. Anne's hair sat atop her head in a sloppy bun and round-rimmed sunglasses hid her face. She hated walking into places because she swore everyone gave her dirty looks. People around Turkeyfoot knew who she was and who her husband was, and it wasn't Case Estes. They headed in and walked back to the cooler where they each grabbed a cold can of pop.

Anne's first dose of dope came courtesy of a dentist. John knocked her front row of teeth in one night. She remembered seeing red and white blot out her eyes. Their relationship had always been volatile, but she knew they really loved each other. She knew in her heart she cherished their marriage even more than Lucy. Her daughter would grow up and leave her. All she had was John Perley. Yet here she was with Case, just to get high for a few days. They piled their crumpled bills and loose change on the countertop to pay the clerk and Case asked for a pack of Kentucky's Best.

CHAPTER FOURTEEN

At suppertime, Lucy played with her toy kitchen set. The girl hummed songs her mother taught her and cooked plastic recipes on a toy stove. She filled a cup with water and placed it on the armrest of the couch where her father had managed to sleep the rest of the day away.

The stale August evening slowly burned out and night fell. Mamaw Perley's tires crumbled the still night as they ascended the long driveway up to the trailer, the headlights beaming through the living-room window. The Cutlass hadn't moved since the day her mother left. Mamaw Perley climbed out of a newer model SUV and carefully walked up the porch steps. When she knocked on the door, Lucy answered. John snored on the couch.

"Are you okay, honey? Has he even fed you anything today?" Mamaw Perley asked.

"I made her some eggs this morning," John groaned from the couch, his eyes still closed.

"That's all she's ate?! And besides, she needs a lot more than just food in her guts! The door ain't even locked. I could've been anybody." Mamaw Perley's cheeks burned and her hands shook slightly as she clutched her oversized purse hanging from her shoulder. "Where's Anne?"

"She left like she always does," John said.

Lucy's grandma's keys jingled in her hand as she pulled the girl by the wrist into the thick night air.

"You'll just come with me till they can get their act together, baby," she told Lucy.

John Perley's head might as well have been glued to the couch. He thought to argue with his mother just for the sake of rustling her up, but figured Lucy would be better off gone anyways. Moths swarmed the porch light outside. He stretched his neck up as far as he could and watched out the window as the headlights backed away and darkness swallowed him.

"You just get done snorting my ring up your damned nose?!"

Sweetie slapped John's face, but the man didn't answer. John's mouth hung open in a frown with drool at the corners. His arms lay flat against his thighs, his palms open to the ceiling. Sweetie smacked him again, harder this time, and John's eyelids struggled to peel back. The dark of his eyes darted all around the room.

"Where'd you sell it at? I know you took it, I had it setting right on the dashboard of the truck!" Sweetie palmed John's greasy head of curls and shook him.

"I ain't sold...nothing," John mumbled and folded his face up into a frown. He slumped over on his side and closed his eyes again. The window behind the couch in John's living room was tacked over with a thick sheet. Sweetie Goodins looked around at the mess. In the kitchen dishes were piled in the sink like small mountains, mold bubbled up in glass valleys and ridges. Notice papers and red slips smothered the coffee table. Drywall crumbled into a pile on the living-room carpet, a hole revealing a bright wooden stud in the shadows of the trailer.

Sweetie gazed down on John Perley. The younger man was small, especially folded up asleep. John's bony chest pushed slow rasps out of his mouth. Sweetie could see a needle folded up in a hankie poking out from underneath the couch. He wiped his hand down his own face and closed the door behind him on his way out.

CHAPTER FIFTEEN

That night at her grandma's, Lucy couldn't hardly sleep. She kept dreaming of her mother spinning the wheels off of cars and birds chirping in the dead of night. Mamaw Perley fell asleep in her recliner watching a black-and-white movie that showed a man with shining, greased-back black hair tightly embracing a young woman in a great blossoming dress. The television flickered light across Lucy's face, but when the girl awoke again, the room was silent and the screen blank. Her granny's chair was empty except for a balled-up quilt. Lucy shut her eyes and prayed for her mother and father to be normal again. She tried to imagine her words floating thin as smoke up to God, far beyond the jagged tree lines at the top of the mountain ridge.

Lucy was all set up on the couch, her very own pile of pillows and a quilt heavier than herself. She listened to herself breathe and tried to lay as still as possible. On the wall across from her hung a clock. It was built in the image of a birdhouse. Every hour the tiny red door clacked open, and a trio of plastic birdies came out to sing their song. But for now, the only sound was its hollow ticktocks.

She stood up from the couch, and her toes sank down into the plush carpet of her granny's double-wide. She stepped into the kitchen and opened the fat chrome refrigerator. Colorful cans of pop lined the door in rows, there were pudding cups, and microwaveable breakfast sausages. Different-named cheeses and thin-cut turkey instead of her daddy's bologna from the corner store. Lucy's face glowed in the blinding fridge light. She took a juice pouch and let the stainless-steel door shut with a sucking sound.

Mamaw lived in a trailer park. Outside, a telephone pole shone a dull orange glow onto the road. Lucy fretted over her father. She wondered who would watch for his raggedy breaths while she sipped on sweet fruit punch in a place that felt a world away, even if it was just uptown a few miles. Lucy had heard kids in school tease others for living in a trailer park, but she liked them. Mamaw Perley's house was always clean and orderly. Outside there was a short driveway and a sturdy front porch lined with bushes that made her feel boxed in and safe.

The kitchen floor was a glossy tile that sure looked like real wood even if it wasn't. It was cold on her bare feet, Lucy felt like she needed to be cautious in this strange place. She watched every move she made, afraid one misstep might shatter this fragile bliss.

Back in the living room, the wooden birds danced and clucked on the hour. Lucy climbed back up to her pile of pillows and settled in underneath the weight of the quilt.

One thing about Lucy's mamaw was that she liked to stay busy. Just about every morning Lucy was there, the smell of cinnamon and vinegar filled the double-wide. If she wasn't baking, she was cleaning. The old woman would wear a loose T-shirt that had a cartoon of a flying pig on the front of it and jeans cinched tight around her soft, wide waist. She scrubbed her kitchen floor viciously with a Brillo pad. The knees of her pants soaked up soapy water as she worked from one end of the kitchen floor to the other. Her bangs hung in her eyes until she pulled herself up straight and pushed them back. She was red faced and short of breath, but she tucked the loose pieces of hair behind her ears and kept working until the entire kitchen was to her liking. When finished, she groaned as she planted one foot and stood up off her knees.

Later in the afternoon, sweat dripped down Mamaw Perley's forehead while she stacked boxes onto the kitchen table. Each was marked off with neon stickers and bold Sharpie; twenty-five cents, fifty cents, a dollar.

Lucy followed behind her with a notebook. The girl scribbled with a blue pen and straightened the bracelet around her wrist.

"That just oughta do it, Mamaw. We got it all."

"Do we now? What about all those boxes in the back of my closet? You forget about them?"

"But I'm tired of doing yard-sale stuff. Can't we take a break?"

"I guess we could. Let's go get us some ice cream from someplace," Mamaw said.

Her grandmother took her out to eat in town. The two of them sat silently across from one another in a Dairy Queen booth.

"You don't like your chicken tenders?" Mamaw asked.

"When can I go back home to Mommy and Daddy?" Lucy didn't look up from her basket of food. She swirled a fry in a Styrofoam cup of gravy.

"Give 'em a couple days and we'll check in. You got to get to school tomorrow though. No more hooky this year. I want you to start off on the right foot," Mamaw Perley said. A woman in an apron wiped the table next to them, her name tag hanging crooked from her uniform. The worker limply slapped the wet rag against the tabletop and smeared soapy water around in a half-hearted circle. Lucy might have enjoyed her mamaw's house, but that didn't make it home.

CHAPTER SIXTEEN

Anne Perley dreamed of her husband kicking his boots off at the kitchen table. The room was pitch dark. She heard John slide his jacket from his shoulders and hang it on the back of the wooden chair. He sat down and pulled a pack of cigarettes from his shirt pocket. The rich smell warmed the cold trailer. Anne sat up from her spot on the couch and stared across the dark room at John. A crib for Lucy sat snugly in the corner of the living room. Their narrow trailer didn't offer as much space as Anne had hoped, but they made it work. The baby's things were next to the crib stacked neatly. Diapers, bottles, blankets, and some things Anne hadn't a clue about. She still felt like a kid herself, fresh out of high school with nothing but her daddy's blessing to move in with the father of her daughter. Anne loved the man sitting in the loose pegged kitchen chair, the wooden legs creaking as he bent double to shed his sweaty socks.

Anne loved him so much she prayed for his downfall: a wreck, a near overdose, a brush in with the law, anything to get John to stop partying and staying high. Anne grew up in a family known as outlaws. She didn't want the same for her Lucy. It had always been the typical drinking and smoking she was used to with John; she could handle that. But lately she knew it was something darker. Sweetie Goodins had a reputation around Turkeyfoot. She had worried about her husband working with him so much.

"Y'all get it finished up?" Anne asked into the darkness.

John didn't answer. The tip of his cigarette flared bright, the shape of his face glowed dimly for a second before he breathed smoke from his lungs and the dark consumed him again. Anne could tell he was high just in that glow. His bangs hung shaggy over his forehead, and she couldn't see the blue in his eyes, just two dark holes that she worried wouldn't catch light ever again.

Anne felt the baby hiccup inside of her. John balanced his cigarette on the edge of the ashtray and raked his hair back with his fingers. Anne's cheeks got hot and she felt her eyebrows crinkle.

"If we're gonna sit here in silence can we at least turn on a light? I'm tired of sitting around in the dark all the damn time," Anne said, raising her voice but lost the edge as the last words snagged in her throat and tears welled up from her deep brown eyes.

John still didn't answer his wife. He picked his cigarette back up and took one last hit, then pulled his socks and boots back on. Standing, he kicked the chair under the table. Anne flinched but choked back tears no matter how bad she wanted to cry out. Her husband mashed his cigarette butt into the ashtray and walked out the front door into the night.

Anne followed John out into the sharp December night. The wooden porch was damp and cold on her bare feet. Wrapping her arms around her stomach, she stood at the edge where the steps led down to the driveway and watched as John's car door slammed shut. The engine turned over into a steady humming. Headlights beamed brightly across the fresh white gravel; in the streams of light she saw the first snowflakes of a cold night fall. John shifted into reverse and backed out of the driveway before disappearing down the road.

Anne looked up for the moon among the clouds; she felt jealous of the treetops, of the way the snowflakes drifted and fell along their branches, blanketing the curves of the slender poplar trees in just the right places. The clouds shone silver as they tread their way across the deep, black space above. She reached up, snipped one out of the sky with her fingers, and held it in her hand.

Anne woke up in the passenger seat of the Astro. Case had parked them in the Save-A-Lot parking lot, the van idling briefly before Case killed the engine. Anne bit down on her lip for a moment and then wiped at her nose with the palm of her hand. She could feel the torn cloth seat against her bare thighs. A cheap tallboy sat open in the center console between them, the can's sweat beads pooling in the cup holder.

"Tim is really trying to push this fentanyl shit if he's giving free samples to John." Case said, noticing that she was awake.

"It's supposed to be potent shit. Liable to kill you if you ain't careful." Anne snorted another Percocet from her lap. She slipped a small plate back beneath the passenger seat and picked at a sore on her arm.

"I don't know what the fuck he wants with John. Probably just nervous about having to move it himself if the old man bucked up on him like you say." Case cranked his neck, sweeping his eyes across the length of the parking lot. He sipped his beer and glanced in the rearview.

"I don't like fucking with Tim. Sweetie's one thing, Tim's coldhearted," Anne said.

"He acts like he owns this whole goddamned town. Goes around thinking everybody owes him something." Case rolled the window down and adjusted the side-view mirror so he could get a wider look at the parking lot behind them. "Quit picking at that, it's only making it worse. You and John been shooting up now too?" Case stopped shifting around to stare at Anne's arm. She flattened her palm over the bright scabs and a green bruise on the inside of her elbow.

"Only when we're running low." Anne looked like her soul had drained out of her eyes in a wash of shame.

"It's a waste doing it any other way," Case said.

"Why don't you mind your damn business?"

"You ain't gotta lie to me. I know it's a better high." He took his cap off and ran his hands through his knotty long hair.

"I'm not like you. I only use this shit because I have to. If I didn't hurt so bad, I'd quit it in an instant," Anne said.

"Tell yourself whatever you want. You're hooked just as bad as me or any other dopehead around here." Case laughed and started the engine again.

"Fuck you!" Anne sobbed and stomped her feet against the floorboard of the van.

"You're crazier than hell." Case downed the rest of his beer and pitched it into the back seat.

"You ain't nothing but a junkie! I don't know why I even called you!" Anne cried.

"Then go on home then! Damn! Ain't nobody forcing you to stay." Case opened another beer and slurped the suds off the top.

She slammed the door behind her and took off walking through the parking lot. *What are you doing to yourself? You have a little girl at home worried sick about you*, Anne thought. She began to cry as she crossed the main road and started following the ditch line towards the mountain. She picked up a piece of slate rock and threw it as the Astro sped by her but missed. The gray stone shattered into several pieces against the road. She just wanted to see Lucy. She figured John and her would still have some fussing to do, but it'd pass over like it always did. She just wanted her little girl.

CHAPTER SEVENTEEN

The inside of John's elbow was swelled up into a purple knot the size of a golf ball. He had missed while shooting up and instead of worrying about an infection he cursed himself for wasting dope like that. He was parked on the backside of the Save-A-Lot. It was mostly deserted at this time of day. He had met Tim down here before, but typically not this early. His legs tickled a little like they did when he got nervous. Or maybe he was just really fiending. He couldn't quite tell the difference anymore. John's guts turned over and he contemplated how much longer he could wait for Tim before he might have to hop the guardrail and squat. He squirmed around some more and tried to ignore it, as there weren't many trees or bushes to hide behind in the back lot of a grocery store.

The only person he had seen was a stock boy who had lingered by the dumpster to smoke a cigarette before heading back in to mop the floors or whatever other menial task his manager would assign him. It was a school day and all the morning traffic had died down for the most part. He thought about Lucy getting on the bus at her mamaw's and hoped she would have a good day. He felt guilty hoping that she'd spend at least a few weeks at her granny's. He didn't know what to do about it though. Lucy deserved better, but they couldn't give it to her.

He checked the clock on the car's dashboard: 9:18 a.m. The small blocky numbers seemed frozen. He felt like he had stared at the back of the grocery store more than he had ever noticed the face of the building. He knew well the yellow-stained cinder blocks, the broad cracks that splintered off from the base up to where the rusty gutters sagged hopelessly.

It had rained the last few days, but today the sun was bright, and the air was thick and sticky. Birds chirped and buzzed around the power lines above. He felt like one of them, ready to spread his wings and soar all around town. Wherever his fluttering heart desired. All he needed was for his guy to show up. It didn't matter who he copped from, they were always late. Just a little pick me up and he'd have his head on straight. In another life, it would have been a fine day to hunt agate rock or sift creek beds for arrowheads. But here he sat, staring at the Save-A-Lot loading dock, and the stock boy coming out for another smoke. *What a punk*, he thought. A sudden taste of envy rose up the back of his throat like bile before he swallowed it back down.

He heard tires pressing over gravel. Sure enough, when he glanced in his rearview mirror, Tim's big Ford pulled up behind him. Everything else left his mind as John excitedly opened the car door and started walking over to get into the truck.

Tim was never much for small talk. He was the paranoid type, so they did their business hurriedly and John was ushered back out of the truck. He crossed the back lot again and slammed his car door shut before settling back into the cloth bench seat of the Olds. Stains covered the passenger seat beside him, and fast-food crumbs rested in the grooves of every seam. Crispy cigarette burns had gathered at his crotch. He mumbled a prayer and turned over the ignition. The engine rattled awake and somewhere under the hood a belt whined. He slid the AC switch over to high. He reached into his shirt pocket and pulled out a wad of aluminum foil. John held the small silver ball delicately in his palm, he gently unraveled a pill from its center. His movements were slow and nervous like someone holding a newborn. Outside of his car the wind sent a shopping bag rolling softly down the alley ahead of him.

The Cutlass' cool air finally kicked in. John carefully tucked the foil into the cup holder then cradled the small green tablet in the center of it. He reached over and unlatched the glove box. He took out a small glass dish, a fresh spoon, and a needle. The dish was a creamy haze of a color with a flaky gold inlay around the edge. He used the butt end of his cigarette lighter to grind the pill into a fine powder on the saucer, the pile of dust that would vanish faster than John could blink if he would just roll the window down and let the breeze pass through. One great gust of wind was all it would take. He could never do it, he was bad sick. He raked it into the spoon before pouring a little water on top of it and heating it with his lighter. He only felt better once every drop was pulled safely into the tip of his syringe. His legs tickled now with anticipation. As soon as he dumped it into a vein on his hand, he felt better. He leaned his head against the steering wheel and rested his eyes a moment.

When John woke up to a paramedic dragging him out onto the pavement, he knew he was going to jail. He looked down to see his legs twisted awkwardly over one another, still half hanging in the floorboard of his car. The EMT pulled him the rest of the way out and laid him down on his back. He could see red lights flashing against the back of the Save-A-Lot and the stock boy was watching by the dumpster. *That little punk called the law*, was all he could keep thinking to himself.

Once they were sure he wasn't dead, the first thing they did was have the sheriff search through his car. John cursed himself for not dying. He knew what was sitting in the car just as well as they did. After they had laid it all out on the hood, the officer gave him the spill on his rights and told him he'd be spending a little while at

Three Forks given his prior warrants. The cuffs dug into John's wrists as they sat him in the back of the cruiser, but he was just grateful to still have a little buzz going. It wouldn't last for long though.

CHAPTER EIGHTEEN

John's cell had glazy off-white walls like cream poured into coffee. The thick paint was cracked and peeled back from the harsh edges of the cinder blocks. Through his cell door he could see young and old men playing cards for bags of chips, as sober as they had been in weeks, or months, maybe years. Beyond the card table was a heavy, steel framed door to a hallway. The door was painted a deep blue, but the handle was cold and silver. Sunlight spilled onto the jailhouse floors. Cracks and pits in the pavement had no place to hide below the prisoners' soles.

Down that hall was what everyone called the wish room, the only space with a large window for the inmates, where they could sit, peer out, and just *wish* they were on the other side. It was a sad joke, but it was all they had. On the other side the sky was blue and clear. There was a tree outside that window. It was thin with only a few odd branches, but it shimmied in the breeze and the men inside knew that the world was still screaming by, even if they could not feel it on their own skin.

John sat up on the edge of his cot. He bounced his knees for a moment and focused on the scabs between his knuckles and near the edge of his wrist. He hardly recognized his hands as he folded them over one another.

With nothing else to do John got in on a game of cards in the common room. The dealer was older than most of the men in Three Forks Regional. The man appeared fragile and drawn up. His hands seemed distorted under the dead fluorescent lights. His knuckles bulged out like pieces of gravel and his fingers stretched out like roots. The old, knotted hands didn't shake when he dealt the cards though, they were just as steady as could be.

"The point of Tonk is to go out clean and leave the other fellers at the table with their mouths hanging open," the old man said, holding his cards loosely.

His thin wrinkled lips hadn't stopped since the guard came around and gave them their breakfast, a cold hard-boiled egg with a somehow even colder cup of black coffee. The old man barely took time to fill his lungs between sentences, his chest so bony it rattled.

"Too many folk want to spend the game pouting about the cards they've been dealt instead of figuring on how to best use what they got." The old man seemed not to care whether his audience responded or not, he was content to keep right on rambling. "Or they get a good hand and all they want to do is sandbag. You can lose real quick sandbagging in this game."

"I think I can figure it out as we go," John said. "What laws you break to end up in here, mister?"

"I'm just an old man stuck in his ways." He smiled and his eyes picked over the cards in his hands.

"I'd say I'm stuck in a rut of my own."

"Y'all boys and girls these days all claim you want lawlessness. No sooner than you've crawled up out of the cradle you're running around, doing dope, disrespecting your mommies and daddies. But you don't know shit. Just slaves to your flesh and the world."

John's nose began to drip. He wiped his forearm across his face and left a streak of blood across his skin. His dried lips cracked as he frowned at the sight of the red smear. He left his cards on the table and found the mirror hanging in his cell. It was not made of glass, only a polished cut of sheet metal, scratched and dented from top to bottom.

He stared cockeyed at himself in the mirror. Hairs tufted around his temples. His neck craned to the side and he could feel a knot in his back from the night before. Blood ran from his nose and trickled over his lips. The reflection of himself was dull and broken. He wished himself back home on Turkeyfoot. Back to a place where the roots of poplar trees shot deep into the soft, muddy hillside and the tree trunks climbed up to swipe at the clouds, round and fat all the way up till the tops stretched out and took a deep breath. The mountaintops where long before John men had fallen into darkness that only a musty jailhouse mirror could reveal. He stepped back to sit on his cot and took a small breath. He tongued the dry roof of his mouth. The cream-colored cinder blocks towered around him; he closed his eyes and felt them leaning in on him. His chest tightened, so heavy with sorrow it felt about ready to pull him down to the cold floor. Outside the skies remained clear blue, still enough for somebody to dip a bucket into. The sun barreled over the hills, the light crossing millions of miles to cut through the thin, lonesome window on John's cell wall, barely more than a slice in the cinder blocks. The gleam caught the shabby mirror and threw the rays into his face.

He lost his sight for a second. He took short heavy breaths and wiped fresh blood from his nose into his hands. Clusters of anguish tumbled over one another working to escape his throat, his face twisted in shame, and tears dripped to the floor in sobs. When he opened his eyes again, the weight of the world seemed to topple around him into dust.

CHAPTER NINETEEN

When Anne got back home the trailer was empty. She figured John had hitched a ride up to the sawmill to work for the day and knew Lucy would be with her mamaw. She started a pot of coffee and looked for their stash box, but John either had it with him or had hidden it elsewhere. She needed to get Lucy back from Mamaw Perley's, but first she wanted to get something from Sweetie to help her calm down. Even if they owed him enough to buy a farm, it didn't hurt to try.

The second she heard wheels hit the driveway Anne got shifty. She peeked out the kitchen window blinds as Sweetie's black truck with windows tinted even darker came to a stop. *Only someone with something to hide has a need for windows that black*, she thought to herself. The truck's thick tire tread was like rows of hungry teeth, and the frame of the vehicle sat perched up off the ground like it was ready to swallow someone up.

The sound of crunching gravel was replaced by the squeaky driver's door letting out a tired groan as Sweetie opened and slammed it back shut. The heel of the old man's boots clicked against the wooden slabs as he strolled up the steps and across the porch. Sweetie wasn't a large man, but when Anne opened the door for him his shadow towered down on her. His hair was slicked to the side with pomade. He smelled like cheap cologne.

"Hot-ass day, ain't it?" Sweetie said. Anne stared at the man's slim silhouette, with his head hung cockeyed.

"I was thinking it was pretty chilly in here. You got any of those thirties?" Anne said.

"Goddamn, that's all you junkies think about. Can't even spare a man a greeting." Sweetie scowled at Anne.

"You know I ain't called you over here to talk about the damned sun sitting in the sky."

Anne stepped aside and let Sweetie into the crisp cool air of the living room. She closed the door and they sat down on the couch in front of the coffee table. Behind them, the air conditioner hummed, tucked snugly into the window.

"Just let me get one of those, and I'll pay you for it once John gets this load of timber at the mill done," Anne Perley said, bouncing her heel.

"You'll pay me for it my ass. How many times have I heard that shit?"

"I only have a twenty-dollar bill to my name. What'd you come over here for anyways if you ain't gonna front me? You know we always stay broke."

"You're gonna have to trade for it then." Sweetie's teeth shone white in the dark living room as he spoke.

Anne went to her bedroom for her jewelry box. It wasn't handmade or anything fancy to look at it. It might have been cherry, but it could just as easily have been made of stained plywood. The box's small drawers were lined with green felt. She kept her rings, necklaces, and earrings divvied up into their own compartments.

Sweetie plucked up a silver chain with a small jewel hanging from it. Anne snapped the box shut and held her last twenty-dollar bill out to the man. He reached into his boots and took out a sandwich baggy of pills. Some were big and some small, some round, and some like rectangles—blue, green and white all mixed together. He pinched one out and tossed it onto the coffee table. It rolled to a stop at the edge. Anne snatched up her plate and started grounding down the pill immediately. Her knee never stopped bouncing while she worked at it.

"At least say a little grace or something." Sweetie shook his head and turned Anne's jewelry over in his palm before stuffing it with the money into his shirt pocket.

She sniffed and hacked to clear her throat after she had snorted the whole pill. Even back when she first met John he was running around with Sweetie Goodins. He tagged along on odd jobs with the older man to buy cheap weed for the weekends when he'd burn the wheels off that ugly old Camaro with black leather seats. Anne had wondered then if the leather seats were genuine; she'd discover they were not. The woman's eyes drooped, almost crossed, and she eased back onto the couch. Sweetie let himself out the front door while Anne dreamed of being young again.

In her dream, Anne's father was drunkenly picking through the garden for a cucumber. She watched him from the front porch. The garden sat at the top of a gentle slope. He was so drunk his eyes had that dead glaze over them and his knees spun beneath him. He told Anne before he went up there that he didn't want a cucumber that was yellow and overripe. He said he'd crawl around all night if that was what it took to find a bright-green one. It was Sunday afternoon, but he was still wearing his Friday-night jeans. Two or three buttons were missing from his shirt causing the hem of it to flap freely about in the breeze. Her dad's hips were sharp and narrow. His muddy work boots swallowed up his ankles.

Anne stepped down from the porch and crossed her driveway. John Perley had just pulled up and was waiting for her. The car was crimson red with rally wheels. White dust from the gravel chalked up its fenders.

"He's feeling good tonight, huh?" John laughed as Anne sat down in the passenger seat.

"He's hunting him a cucumber for supper. Once he's got that squared away, he'll be all set," she said.

Anne's face was caked with makeup and her nails had been painted red days ago, but now they were chipped up and flaky. Her hair was like brown springs.

"Let's go down to the lock," John said.

He shifted the car into reverse and flipped them around. A tree limb brushed the roof of the car as they passed through the metal gate and slowly bounced down the long gravel road. Anne watched her father in the rearview mirror as he plopped down at the bottom of the hill and turned a big green cucumber over in his palms. The tires squealed as the Camaro pulled out onto pavement. John rolled down the window and the wind slapped at the young couple's faces.

When they got to the lock, they watched the water rushing over and down past the bend of the river. Trash and worn-down tires bobbed and gasped for breath, caught in the wash. John took out a joint. It was fat on one end and narrowed out to a spindly twist. Anne's chipped nails clicked around inside her purse before she pulled out a lighter. Anne pinched the twisted paper between her teeth and held the BIC's flame to the rounded end. The paper smoldered black. Above the river, trees exploded against the off-blue sky in different shades of green. A haze hung in the air. The wind combed through the treetops. Anne wanted John to run his fingers through her hair much the same.

The river and the earth and the treetops all piled on top of one another. Anne rubbed at her eyes and gripped the seat below her thighs. Her face felt red-hot as she passed the joint back to John.

She watched the trash struggle to swim again where the river tripped over the lock. Crumbling concrete walls and pitting steel jutted out of the stream. The water didn't draw deep breaths like John and Anne, the only mercy it knew was God's. It cut a path with force and didn't look back with regret or feel the shame that came with drowning those in its path. Gray plumes of clouds swirled above the hot-rod coupe and its two lovers. Branches whipped and cracked. The leaves were hopeless against the heavy winds that dipped into the mountain valley. The leaves held tight to life, they did not scream, and they did not beg. They grasped at their branches harder than they did when the sun shined, and no matter how deep Anne looked into herself, she would never understand what kept them from letting go. It would be easier to give in, she had thought. To flip in the breeze and sink under the river to where the current pulled them, and a leaf never shined green in the light of day again.

The drive home was blurry until the tires left the pavement and clawed back up Anne's driveway. The car's oil pan almost bottomed out as it scraped across a gravel rut. Anne felt her buzz do the same. The limbs brushed the top of John's car again as they passed through the rusty gate and turned to meet the small farmhouse. The siding was faded white and the porch seemed to sag in on itself.

John cut the engine and Anne's ears were filled with the hum of cicadas settling in for the evening. They crossed the porch and stepped into the living room. Anne's father was sprawled out on the couch asleep. An ashtray spilled out next to him. He was still in his dirty jeans. On the coffee table was his open pocketknife and half of a bright-green cucumber. Anne glanced down at her father and then back to John before heading towards the hallway.

The floor creaked under John's boots as he followed her through the house and into her room.

His thighs felt hot and sticky against her own. She held her breath and listened as his chest gently rose in the dark room. She thought of her father in the living room alone. She wondered if he had cleaned up his spilt cigarette ash or eaten the rest of his cucumber. Anne wondered if he was even breathing at all.

She woke up in a panic. She didn't know how long she had slept, but she hadn't heard a sound from Lucy. She was already down the hall and turning the handle to her daughter's bedroom before it struck her that Lucy wasn't home. She still needed to call John's mother. She tried to steady her breathing, but it felt hard to believe that this was her life. Mamaw Perley picked up on the first ring.

"Honey, you've had me worried sick," Mamaw Perley said as soon as she answered.

"Is Lucy okay?"

"She's fine. That foolish son of mine ain't though." Mamaw Perley was getting wound up as she spoke without taking a breath. "He called me from up there at the jail. I got the money for his bail if you want to get him, but I ain't going. I told him I don't even want to hear his voice on the phone. Lucy's fine right where she's at. I'll bring her by when she's ready."

"I'll be over there," Anne said.

"I'll put it in the mailbox. Take care of yourselves, please. This little girl needs y'all."

Anne's head was still at the river in her haze of a dream. Those first dates with John felt like it hadn't been so long ago. It had been summertime then too. She knew they had to change, but she didn't know where to begin. They needed to get away.

CHAPTER TWENTY

"I'm so glad to see you." John hugged Anne tightly, pulling her up by the waist.

"Fuck you. We ain't got bond money. We're gonna owe your mother for a year after this," Anne said, struggling from his grip and pushing him away.

"She'll be okay, y'all had to get me out. I gotta get back to work if we aim to make any headway." John hopped into the passenger side of the Oldsmobile while Anne walked back around to drive.

"I hope it was worth it. We paid damn near three grand for that pill." Anne drove with both hands squeezing the steering wheel as she spoke.

"Those other charges are bullshit. I didn't have near as much on me as they're saying I did."

"It doesn't matter, they're the law!"

"Quit tailgating these people, fuck," John said.

Anne slammed the brakes and the Cutlass skidded over into the other lane to a stop. An oncoming car screeched to a halt and blared on its horn before racing its engine and cutting around them on the shoulder.

"Have you lost your fucking mind!" John had his palms planted firmly against the dashboard.

"Lucy has been sitting all alone because all you give a damn about is yourself!" Anne was shaking all over.

"Don't you act all high and mighty on me. You would've been right there with me if you weren't out fucking half the mountain for a fix. Don't start that shit with me!" John punched the dashboard and the cheap plastic cracked open. Anne balled her tiny fist and wailed on the side of John's face and shoulder, but the blows barely phased him. He grabbed her wrist and curled it back until she stopped fighting against him.

"Please, honey. Let me drive if you want, but let's get home before we both get sent right back up there," John said. "We can fight about this anytime, but not here in the middle of the road."

Anne cut the wheel back over the yellow line and mashed the gas to the floor. The big white car's carburetor wailed down the road like a growing storm. The Perleys stared ahead, their jaws locked in silence.

CHAPTER TWENTY-ONE

The sky was mostly clear, but what clouds did float overhead spat cold hard drops of rain down around Sweetie Goodins. The moon was full and shining above. His dreams were filled with his father and harvest days on the farm. His young body aching, hacking down tobacco plants with a hatchet, stacking them on the spear, and hanging them up to dry in the barn. Afterwards he'd taste his mother's iced lemonade again. He'd give anything to do it once more, but at the time he hated it with everything in his gut. That was all gone now. That world had passed away from him and when he went back into the house to sleep, he ached in a new way.

Sweetie startled awake to silence and the sunrise. His

father had been sleeping later and later, but never until after daybreak. There was no shuffling about in the living room. The smell of the furnace was gone from the night before. Sweetie jumped out of bed in his underwear and rushed into the front room. The old man was slumped over by the kitchen table, but his chest still rose with shallow breaths.

Sweetie ran back to his room and put pants on. He cinched his belt tight and hurried to scoop his father out of the floor. Sweetie struggled at his age, but the old man had lost a lot of weight so he managed to half carry and half drag him out to the truck. He didn't bother calling an ambulance. He figured he was faster than that.

The thought occurred to Sweetie that maybe he should let the old man move on. His father was all he had, but it wasn't his decision to make.

"I'm fine, damn it! Turn around and go home." His father had come around as they neared town.

"You ain't fine."

"They're gonna have me put away over nothing, son."

"Let's just see what they say."

"You should've just let me be."

His father turned out to be sort of right. The old man had suffered a minor stroke. The hospital couldn't force him to do anything, but suggested rehab if he still wanted to be able to get around on his own.

"It'll only be a little while," Sweetie said.

"You should've left me lying there."

"Your Medicare ought to cover it at the county nursing home."

"Should've let me die at home."

CHAPTER TWENTY-TWO

Sweetie combed pomade through his thick peppered hair. The bathroom mirror was foggy, though he still stared into it. He wiped his palm across and left a wide streak in the condensation. His eyes were gray in the mirror, his hair shone on top of his head, and sweat beaded up on his forehead.

In the kitchen, Sweetie's cell phone rang. The prepaid flip phone rattled on top of the kitchen table. Sweetie didn't recognize the number so he let it go to voicemail. When he played the recording, John's voice crackled in his ear. Sweetie shook his head and dropped the phone into his shirt pocket, then finished getting dressed. On the drive to the nursing home his father was chattier than usual.

"I just wished to go to church service one last time before I had to come up here. I would've liked to make sure I'm in good standing with the Lord," Sweetie's father said.

"Why now?" Sweetie asked.

"Don't play dumb with me, I know once I get checked in up there my chances coming out alive are gone."

"I ain't never heard you ask to go in all these years. We could've gone any Sunday."

"I just ain't been ready."

"I'm sure they'll have something for y'all up here."

"I'm gonna need you to bring me my water by too."

"I know for a fact they got clean water up here. You're in the middle of damn town," Sweetie said.

"I can't drink it. It ain't my spring water. It's like to poison me."

They parked right in front. His father shuffled hesitantly through the sliding-glass doors. They come to face Mamaw Perley turning from the receptionist.

"Howdy, ma'am. How's John and Anne doing?" Sweetie asked.

"They won't hardly do nothing anymore. I keep Lucy half the time," she said.

"That's probably for the better. Have you seen the filth they have that baby girl living in up there?"

"Well, I'm her grandmother, Mr. Goodins. I reckon I have."

"I just hate it for her is all," Sweetie said.

"I don't see how you have much to say about any of it considering your role in the situation." Mamaw Perley waited for Sweetie to respond, but he clasped his mouth shut tight. "Yes, I know what goes on up on that mountain. Have you found a conscience all of a sudden, Mr. Goodins?"

"Well, it was good talking to you. I'm sorry I said anything." Sweetie turned and led his father onward. The woman marched out into the parking lot with the doors closing behind her like the Red Sea. Sweetie's ears burned more with each step he took as Mamaw Perley's words settled over him.

CHAPTER TWENTY-THREE

Sweetie crumbled a Dairy Queen biscuit over a plate of gravy and eggs. He'd been trying to stay away from the house since dropping his father off at the nursing home. He took his plastic spoon, stirred the flaky pieces of bread over, and then tore the corner off a packet of pepper. In his coffee he added half-and-half, stirring it slowly while chewing a bite of fried egg. Somewhere behind the counter the morning manager barked orders at a worker, telling him to wipe down the ice machine.

Sweetie's hat lay next to him in the seat of his booth. He was alone, but a small group of men his age gathered at the far end of the restaurant. He listened to them mumble about the weather and where their taxes were going. One of them wore a polo shirt with the collar stretched around his fat neck, a big garnet class ring nestled between two wrinkly knuckles. Another's hat was bigger than his head—it sat way back off his forehead and Sweetie wondered how he kept it from sliding right off onto the floor. On his way out to his truck, Sweetie waved to the woman working the counter and wished her a good day.

Town had yet to warm to life as Sweetie's brakes squealed and his truck came to a stop at the red light in front of the courthouse. The constable's cruiser sat parked on the curb out front of the building's steps. Sweetie's eyes darted across the street to where most of the storefronts were boarded up, all but a bright-green payday lender's window that had bold yellow print screaming MONEY NOW and FIRST LOAN FREE at any folk pitiful enough to believe it. The light cycled back to green, and Sweetie let his foot off the brake, the truck slowly rolling forward. Fog was beginning to lift from the sidewalks and soon school buses would begin heading out on their morning routes.

Fishing had been one of the few things Sweetie prided himself on. He wasn't a wise farmer like his father or skilled with machines as his older brother had been. But he could bait a hook and knew just when to set it. Sweetie liked to run two hooks off a single line, and more than once had dragged in a pair of catfish together. When he was young, he didn't care to head down to the river to sit for a while. Or if he knew of a secluded fishing spot on someone's property, he still had the muster to make the hike to it. But now in his older days he had grown tired of cutting lines tangled up on river debris, and at the pay lake there was no one to bother him or run him off their land.

Sweetie straddled the yellow line to pass a mail carrier, and then returned to his side of the road. The houses that he passed were structures from another decade, yellow and brown paneling, some with brick walls brought together by an entire side of pane glass. An old Crown Victoria sat in one of the driveways—every winter an old woman would come out and fasten a tarp around its square metallic body.

Through the next red light, the neighborhoods dwindled and the tree lines came back into view. As Sweetie topped the last crest of a hill on his way out of town, a white box truck stood against the horizon and its rising sun. The sky's colors were muted overhead, the cool morning prepared to turn stale with dry autumn heat. Sweetie was grateful he packed a cooler before heading down to the pay lake. Today was the day they'd stock more fish. Sweetie would settle in for an hour or two before the truck arrived, but eventually he'd hear its low chugging engine climb the gravel road and pull up alongside the sheet-metal chute that dipped into the small pond. Several hundred pounds of channel cats would come sliding and shimmying out at once on their way into a new prison.

The road became narrow and the potholes deeper. Sweetie tightened his wrist as he drove through a steep curve where the pavement branched off upward into a sloping pebble path winding around a dull bank before the treetops opened to the pay lake. Dry brown dirt and slate rock surrounded the small hole of water. A couple of old men had already beaten him to the best spots. Sweetie parked his truck in front of a small wooden shack, its rickety steps rose up to a shabby front porch perched above a steep bank where the water gleamed below. A hand-painted sign read NO DRUGS OR ALCOHOL in bold black letters. Sweetie wiped his boots on the doormat and a bell clinked dully when he entered. Inside the shack stood a row of sparsely stocked shelves with canned beanie weenies and candy bars, like a gas station short on supply. A bright-blue minifridge with a glass door had glowing Pepsi logos on its sides.

"You aiming to try it today, Sweetie?" the man behind the counter said. He hooked a finger into his lip and plopped a wad of soggy chewing tobacco out into his hand that he then slung into the trash can before wiping his palm on his jeans.

"I reckon I'll take a go at it. Y'all stocking today?" Sweetie asked.

"They oughta be here with a truckload about noon or so. You know how they are though, always running late." A jar full of crumpled dollar bills with a piece of paper taped across it was labeled TAG FISH. Sweetie signed his name on a clipboard and stuffed a bill through the slit in the top of the plastic lid.

"Well, good luck down there. Holler if you need anything," the owner said before packing his lip tight with more chewing tobacco.

Ripples of white light danced across the surface of the

water. Sweetie's bobber floated stiffly in a shady corner where tree roots gnarled out of the sharp broken bank. The only other two men sat opposite from Sweetie, out of earshot. He rummaged through coats and trash piled behind the seat of his truck until he found what he was looking for. A clear bottle with the label shredded mostly off. Sweetie took a small pull. The clear liquor burned the back of his throat and he coughed before tossing it back into the littered floorboard. He didn't drink much, but he didn't mind on a day like today. *Moderation.* The word formed in his mind. That was one of the things that got under his skin the most about the folks he served endlessly. They came at all times, every day of the week, completely ravenous. No idea of how to enjoy just a taste of something, to savor something instead of having at it until it meant absolutely nothing.

Just then Sweetie saw the rusting white hood of the Perleys' Oldsmobile crawling over the hilltop from the road. Two heads bobbled next to each other on the way down. They slowly crept past the shack and came rounding the curve of the water bank towards Sweetie's spot. The two men on the other side of the lake craned their necks to look and then refocused on their bobbers, unwilling to give their day of peace to these unwelcomed strangers. Sweetie groaned as he stood up from his poles and recognized John behind the wheel. John knew good and well that he hated when they came around like this while he was trying to fish. *They're going to get me ran off from the one good spot on Turkeyfoot*, he thought to himself. Sweetie had long been suspicious that they showed up at places like this on purpose so he'd try to get rid of them quicker, whether they had the money for him or not. John pulled the Cutlass' grill up until it almost kissed the bumper of his truck. Sweetie realized it was Anne in the car with him. The Lucy girl must have been in school. The Cutlass' fender was dented in, the brick headlights foggy and pale in the morning light, like two eyes fixed in a dead man's head.

"How did you know I was up here?" Sweetie asked before John's window was even rolled down all the way.

"Seen you drive by, just figured this was where you were heading. Say, you got any of those things?"

"Is that all you two ever do?" Sweetie's eyes fell to a fresh sore in the crook of John's elbow. "You two been shooting this junk?"

"You ain't seen Tim any, have you?" John pulled his hoodie sleeves down to his wrists to cover his track marks. The banged-up Oldsmobile idled loudly, somewhere inside the engine a piston knocked, the seats were torn at the sides, and the dashboard sported a wide crack down the center that branched out the closer it got to the windshield.

"No. He's been doing a lot more deals on his own," Sweetie said. "Fooling with that synthetic shit. He won't hardly pick up the phone when I call anymore."

"I've heard it's some mean stuff, got people killing over." John wiped his mouth and looked across the pay lake at one of the other fishermen. Anne wiped at her nose with her hand and picked at a sore on her arm.

"He said anything to you about it at the mill?" Sweetie

cranked his neck around, sweeping his eyes across the length of the pond. John fidgeted and glanced in the rearview mirror.

"I wouldn't piss on Tim's feet if they were on fire. He ain't got no business with us anyways. Fuck him," Anne said. She wiped blood from her scab with a wad of tissue. Sweetie could tell she was already fully loaded.

"Quit picking at that," John snapped at her.

"You two are going to end up just like those Estes boys if y'all keep shooting this shit up your arm. They don't care about a thing anymore. Every time I see Case, he's either crying and carrying on about how rough he has it or he's mean as a copperhead. Nothing in-between."

John shifted around in his seat. Sweetie stared at Anne's arm, but she didn't bother trying to hide it like John had.

"How's that Oldsmobile running? It's sounding rough."

"Transmission is slipping some, but it gets us around just fine. Say, you got any of those thirties or not? You got anything on you?"

"Give me a minute."

Sweetie walked back to the water away from their car, he crouched at the bank and splashed water over his wrists and palms. He wiped them together and dipped them into the water again. Slime and night-crawler guts smeared off until only clear droplets trickled down the backs of his hands, like small pearls shattering when they fell to the dirt, leaving a spotted trail behind him as he walked back up to his truck. Sweetie opened the door and reached under the driver's seat, his forearm pressed against the cold metal of the seat adjuster bar, he stretched his fingertips back until he pinched the corner of the plastic bag and dragged the pills out. He peered into the ziplock and removed two Oxycodone. A line ran down the center of each small green tablet, perfect little circles with an M stamped into them. He closed them tight in his fist and stepped back over to the window of John's car.

"Sweetie, we're broke today, but we can get you back later this week for these," John said.

"Just get the hell out of here before you get all three of us run off. How many times do I have to tell you not to come up here when I'm fishing?"

"I know, I know! We appreciate it, man. We'll let you get back to it. Good luck."

Sweetie looked at his hands as the Perleys' car rounded back the other way beyond the pond, disappearing over the hillside. Mud darkened the edges of Sweetie's fingernails. A smell like rotten moss rose from the edge of the pond. Sweetie reeled his pole back in to check the bait and found only a shiny empty hook on the end of his line.

"Sorry fools cost me my only bite this morning," he mumbled to himself.

He snatched a plump night crawler out of a coffee can in the bed of his truck. He held the worm tight between his thumb and forefinger then threaded it onto the barbed end of the fishing hook. The sun had risen higher now, his forearms burned under its light, but it was a welcomed sting. A fish rolled with a splash over the surface of the water. By the time he focused, only ripples faded from the center of the lake. On the hillside a dog slept under the shade of a tree. Sweetie cast his line towards a foamy corner of the pond, where his bobber rocked back and forth. The bright orange tip teetered before settling into balance. He rested his reel in the dust at his boots and walked back to the truck where he took a pop out of his cooler. He pulled the tab and touched the cool wet side of the can to his cheek before taking a long drink.

Sweetie listened to the silence under the dead heat of the climbing morning sun. Nothing was eager to stir in such thick air. He reached down with one hand and winded the reel until the slack in the line pulled tautly. Then he crouched down onto his heels and watched the breeze toss the water back and forth.

CHAPTER TWENTY-FOUR

Sweetie grew restless waiting. With an hour until the stock truck was scheduled to come, he saw his orange floater had just leaned sharply and plunged about halfway underwater. His hands scrambled for the reel. After a strong pull, he knew he'd hooked it. He began reeling some and pulling, reeling and pulling, until he started to make ground with it. The fish rolled closer to the bank desperately trying to break free, but Sweetie walked around the edge of the bank closer to where it struggled. He had almost guided it to a muddy spot where the water had dried up, when he heard wheels spinning against gravel and throwing dust on the hill. He glanced up to see the hood of the Cutlass bounce over a rut in the driveway and come speeding around the dirt road towards him. The line twanged and popped and went slack and Sweetie knew he just lost his only fish of the day.

"You worthless son of a bitch," Sweetie mumbled through gritted teeth at the car window. John rolled it down and Sweetie could see pure panic in the younger man's eyes. More awake than Sweetie had known him to be in a long while.

"Anne is dying. We got to do something for her," John said.

"What the hell you talking about?!" Sweetie's jaw popped he held it so tight.

"We was shooting what you gave us and then took some of the synthetic stuff on top of it and she went out like a light. Follow me up to the house. I don't know what to do for her, Sweetie."

"She's probably just knocked out drooling like y'all always do. Calm down."

"No, Sweetie, no. It's not like that. I've never seen her like this, you know we've been hooked on this shit a long time. She ain't right."

Sweetie glanced around the pay lake. One man had just packed up and gone home, the other shook his head at the water. Dust was still settling from the Cutlass speeding over the hill.

"I'll follow you out." Sweetie could feel his stomach sink inside of him.

John shifted his car down into gear and took off again. Sweetie watched him bottom out at the ridge, the tires spun in the dirt for a minute and then he was gone. Sweetie threw his reel in the back of the truck and slammed up his tailgate with his tackle box still hanging open. Up the hill, the old man from the shack stood on the porch with his hands in his pockets. Sweetie stopped and rolled the window down to hear what he had to say.

"I don't care about your personal business, but don't bring it up here." The man spat an amber arc of tobacco juice out into the gravel. Sweetie just waved and nodded and gunned it up the rest of the hill where the road curled back down to pavement. He cut out towards the Perleys' driveway with his truck engine whistling and the poplar trees blurring together.

Anne was dead on the couch when Sweetie walked through the doorway. John had been right there next to her with his own eyes rolled back. Like two little lovebirds floating along. But now the world was sharp again. The pills had worn off and there was only a lonesome man and no song left to sing. Just the broken-down couch in their living room, same as when they got married. A smell like cat piss and burnt matches hung in the air.

John pushed the coffee table away from the couch and got down on his knees by his wife. Her hips were sharp beneath a pair of thin denim shorts, her arms positioned awkwardly at each side with her mouth half opened like she wanted to say something. Her cheeks drooped like two gaping sinkholes opening into her face. Sweetie sat down at the kitchen table, grateful that at least her eyes were closed. John cried into her lap, occasionally lifting his head and scanning her body up and down like he was looking for some sign of life he had overlooked before. John's mouth opened to say something but snapped back shut. Sweetie's eyes flatly fell to the corpse now, like a stain needing removal. He tried to swallow, but his throat was tight and dry. He found it hard to believe just a few hours ago he was enjoying breakfast alone. He stood up from his seat in the kitchen and his shadow hugged John's shoulders.

"Grab her," Sweetie said.

"What do you mean?" John asked. He looked up from the floor, his eyes swollen red with tears.

"Grab her up and let's get her out of here," Sweetie said.

John's face twisted in disgust at Sweetie's words. "Grab her up? She ain't a piece of roadkill, this is my wife. We can't just dump her off somewhere like a damned piece of trash." John bolted up from his knees.

"You asked for my help, this is what we do. She's been gone, ain't she? Off running around with God knows who? She partied a little too hard this time and never came home. You don't know shit and you damn sure didn't see me today. Got it?!" Sweetie grabbed John by his cheeks and pulled him in close until their foreheads touched. John dropped his eyes to the floor.

"What do you want to do with her? Shouldn't we just call an ambulance? Ain't it illegal to arrest someone if they call for an overdose? Let's just call them, Sweetie."

"If you wanted to get the law involved you should've never come and drug me down here. I just wanted to spend a morning fishing, boy. I'm here now, we're doing it my way."

The men stared eye to eye now. Sweetie's denim button-up shirt was stark blue, piercing in the dark room. John's tears began again, but this time his jaw was locked shut in anger.

"Where's the girl?"

"Who?"

"Lucy! Your daughter, you fucking fool!"

"She's at school, but her granny's picking her up."

"When will she be home?"

"Probably later tonight or tomorrow morning."

"Okay. Put some shoes on her, grab her purse, get her in the car. I'll follow you up to the lock. Don't stop for nothing." Sweetie waited for an answer, but the younger man could only choke back sobs.

"You hear me, dumbass?" Sweetie asked.

"And then what?" John looked back at his wife's lifeless body on the couch.

"And then we let someone else find her. I have no desire to answer all the questions the law is going to have." With one hand Sweetie grabbed the sleeve of John's shirt and pulled him back around to face him.

"Do you?" Sweetie asked.

"No."

"And clean all this shit up." Sweetie gave the coffee table a kick with his boot, and something rattled: Anne and John's kit. A dirty tablespoon and a needle clanked together, a cotton ball and a lighter lay side by side next to a box of matches and a burnt-down candle. Sweetie scowled at John whose eyes were fixed on a pill left in the center of a porcelain dish.

"We were going to split that once we woke up." Tears welled again in the corner of his eyes. "We didn't want to end up like this you know, Sweetie? This wasn't exactly the plan."

Sweetie didn't care what John had to say, he stepped outside to wait. The sun had peaked overhead now and he thought about the channel cats squirming their way down the metal slide into the muddy water. They'd roll around on the surface for a spell before settling into the mud somewhere at the bottom. They'd get hungry and start to stir this evening when it cooled down some. He wondered if the old man would let him throw a line in without paying again. A lousy six-fish limit and a man was expected to release the big ones back in. It was barely enough meat to get stuck between two teeth if someone wanted to take them home and skin them, more fry batter in the pan than fish. Sweetie kicked the toe of his boot against a plank in the porch railing and wondered what was taking John so long. He stepped down into the driveway and opened his truck door. Finding the bag of Oxycodone and Percocet, Sweetie scanned the bed of his truck for somewhere better to stash it, deciding on a bumper jack. He rolled the bag up into a cylinder and used a tire iron to stuff the pills into the hollow metal jack.

John came through the doorway cradling his wife in his arms, carefully sidestepping down the porch stairs. Sweetie turned away while John struggled to put her down in the back seat of the car. The poplars stood straight and still between Sweetie and the sky above—they made a line between him and the road beyond. He watched for the tops to sway in the wind, but the breeze had died down. Green leaves and blue sky overlapped one another. Their bark was gray and dry and thick with age but unbroken on the surface. They towered up stiff in the soil they'd sprouted from.

John took a jacket and spread it out over Anne's face and torso. The waist of the man's work coat came down to her knees, leaving the rest of her legs in the open. John carefully tucked them in, then gently shut the door.

"You ready?" Sweetie asked.

"If we're going to do this, let's get it over with."

Sweetie watched John round the hood of the car and sit down in the driver's seat. The man thumped his forehead against the steering wheel three times and then grabbed the wheel with both hands. A muffled scream came from inside before the rattling engine cranked over. Sweetie climbed up into his truck and waited for John to back out.

As they pulled onto the road, Sweetie checked his rearview mirror. They passed his father's favorite spring on the way up the ridge. When the road began to wind back down towards the river, the paved blacktop turned to dusty gravel at the county line. He thought of his mother's words after a hot day when they'd sit on the porch at home, a watermelon cut up to eat, ice jingling in cups of lemonade, sweat dripping from every crease of his body. The promise of rain and a cool breeze teasing them over the treetops. Sweetie would sit at the bottom step of the porch with his legs spread wide and his shoulders hunched over, picking blades of grass out of the ground between his fingertips.

"We're like a forgotten city up here," his mother would say.

Sweetie's eyes followed the Oldsmobile's broad trunk amidst the dust that rolled up and engulfed the tail end of the car. As they rounded the final curve, Sweetie prayed that nobody was camping or fishing. The gravel path turned into a dirt road with deep muddy ruts that steeped down to the riverbank until the broken cement of the lock's foundation began. John pulled his car up parallel to the top of the lock where the water was calm, small pockets gently swirling together before being sucked over the fall twenty feet below where white foaming suds spat up from beneath. Sweetie shifted the truck up into park and stomped the emergency break to the floorboard. The heat had broken, and the wind had picked up again. When Sweetie stepped out of his truck, the earth near the bank was soft and damp underfoot.

CHAPTER TWENTY-FIVE

They laid Anne's body out facing the crying gray sky. If she were still alive she would feel the pebbles stabbing into her lower back and the coarse slab pricking beneath her shoulder blades. The sound of the river roared around the three as it cut through Lock 13. The massive steel gates had rusted red with disuse. Chunks of concrete crumbled away from the edges into the river below where the water toppled over the man-made structure in a crash before smoothing back out down the bend. Bald tires, lost toys and milk jugs bobbed together in clusters, trapped in the foaming plunge.

Fat raindrops began to snap as the ground was pelted around the two men. Anne's shirt and jeans darkened under the shower. The rain splashed against her face but did not sting anymore.

"I can't just leave her down here in the rain." John's hands trembled at his sides.

"She's dead, John. Sooner or later somebody's gonna want to know where the pill pile that killed her is. Let's make it later."

"Come on now, Sweetie. Help me get her back in the car. Please, I'm begging you!" John sobbed. Sweetie turned and began walking back up from the riverbank to his truck.

"It wouldn't be the first time you've begged me for something, would it? I ain't helping you do shit," he said with his back to John.

John took a few long strides and was on top of the older man. He squeezed him into a headlock and dropped his weight to the ground, dragging Sweetie with him. They rolled in the mud until John got his hands around Sweetie's throat, digging grimy nails into the flesh.

"You got us hooked on these godforsaken pills and you've done killed us both!"

Sweetie's head throbbed and his eyes swelled inside his skull. He kneed John in the groin and scrambled to stand up.

"Get off me, you junkie!"

He struggled for a second with his back pocket before whipping out his snake pistol and pointing it at John, who was still in the mud doubled up like a newborn.

"I didn't kill that girl. Best get that clear in your head."

The heels of Sweetie's boots sank into the mud as he backed towards his truck.

Sweetie slammed his door shut and turned the windshield wipers on. Sheets of rainwater began to cascade over the black Chevrolet. Water slashed ruts into the curves of Turkeyfoot Mountain as it gushed towards the river's edge. Sweetie's truck tires spun softly before catching traction and lurching up onto the narrow dirt road. Sweetie could hardly see the way ahead. All he cared to do was put the river, the Perley family, and the pills behind him for good.

CHAPTER TWENTY-SIX

By the time Sweetie made it back to town the after-school traffic had started. He waited in lines of vehicles while buses made their way out of the high school. Teenagers in lifted trucks blew black smoke out of their exhausts as they peeled out for the weekend. A resource officer stood in the turning lane with a reflective vest and a rain jacket over his uniform, flagging traffic through. Sweetie nodded to the man as he passed by. His tools rattled in the bed over a speed bump. He cut down Main Street back towards the Dairy Queen. The heavy droplets of rain pounded against his windshield as he cut the truck off, the wiper blades stopping in their tracks. He hurried to slide a few quarters into a newsstand box out front, shielding the paper under his armpit before stepping inside to the counter for a coffee. At his booth, he stirred in his half-and-half while unfolding the paper in front of him. The morning crowd had gone on with their day—no more farmers and retired busybodies, the restaurant mostly empty now. Sweetie stared at the ink on the page in front of him, the headlines all blurring together. Anne's body must have been soaked by now, he figured, but someone would find her soon enough. It might take a little longer with the rain, but once it cleared up someone would surely be up there.

CHAPTER TWENTY-SEVEN

When Lucy came home that night the coffee table was wiped clean, and the floor was vacuumed. For the first time in months, the sink was empty of dirty dishes and the shades were pulled back. Her father sat smoking at the kitchen table with an ashtray in front of him. Lucy ran to John and hugged him tight, her arms stretching as far as they could around his rib cage. He ruffled her hair and twisted in his chair to face her.

"Did you have fun at Mamaw's?"

"After school we went to church and I got to play games with the other kids. A lot of them were too little though," Lucy said. "Is Mommy still gone?"

John nodded his head and hugged his daughter up

into his lap. Mamaw Perley walked through the doorway carrying Lucy's backpack.

"Go onto your room while I talk to Mamaw for a minute." Lucy snatched the pink bag and gave her grandmother a hug before prancing back to the hallway, stopping to eavesdrop. John stood and turned his back to his mother. He leaned with his palms flat on the kitchen counter.

"I need some money or they're gonna cut off the electric. You know I don't care about it, but that ain't no good for Lucy," John said.

"Where's Anne?"

"Probably out whoring around with Case as far as I know."

"Watch your mouth. She just bailed you out, y'all are already fighting again?" Mamaw asked.

"I've tried to tell you she's crazy. I'm sure she's somewhere, doped up, cross-eyed, doing just fine, Mom." John's eyes burned into the kitchen counter where he stood with his head drooped between his shoulders. He sucked his cheeks in against his teeth and tapped his foot against the floor.

"Will you please leave, if you ain't going to help us any?" he said.

Mamaw Perley crumpled up a hundred-dollar bill from her purse and pitched it on the counter into her son's gaze. Her face flushed red, and she thought to curse and scream at him, but bit her tongue.

"Go get the electric paid then. Or snort that up too. Not like I can stop you anyhow." Lucy watched her father as he picked up the bill and smoothed it out on the edge of the counter. He folded it in half and tucked it into his shirt pocket.

"Lucy needs to stay with you for a little while longer. That alright?" John said.

"She can move on in as far as I'm concerned. I'll grab her some clothes."

"I don't want to stay at Mamaw's though. I want to see Mommy when she gets home," Lucy said. The girl stood at the edge of the hallway with her backpack hanging at her side in one hand.

"I don't know when your mommy is coming home and I have to work, honey. Just for a few nights, I promise. Come over here."

Mamaw Perley passed Lucy by in the hallway and went about packing the child's things in the back bedroom. Lucy walked to her father in the kitchen. John crouched and cradled her head in his hand as he pulled her into his chest and kissed the crown of her brown hair. He thought about how much she reminded him of Anne. He'd always taken it for granted. Now Anne was all he could see, and she felt so fragile in his grip. He didn't know what was going to come in the next few days, but he knew somebody would report his wife's body soon. There would have to be a funeral. And then the questions would come.

CHAPTER TWENTY-EIGHT

John decided on a cremation immediately. He didn't think Anne would have really minded and it was the cheapest option. Lucy and him had a small visitation before it took place so that the girl could have some closure and see her mother one last time. They had cleaned her up a lot since John last seen her at the riverbank. The funeral home had put her in a yellow dress that John didn't think she'd care for, but seeing as how his mother's church was paying for everything he didn't argue any. Anne's eye sockets seemed fuller, and her skin was warmer, at least at a glance. She was still cold to the touch.

"I miss her," Lucy said.

"I do too."

"Do you think she's happy now?" Lucy asked her father.
"I think she's probably glad to get some rest, baby."

More people came to see her than John had anticipated. Some of the church folk from his mother's congregation brought casseroles for him and Lucy. They placed flower stands and quilts and wind chimes around the casket. The officers who contacted him about her body came dressed in uniform to pay their respects. It made John nervous at first, but they only expressed their condolences. There were others in and out that he assumed were distant relatives and old high school classmates, but he didn't make a point to talk to any of them. The preacher was a broad-shouldered man with a high-and-tight haircut. He wore thick plastic glasses and squeezed John's hand when he shook it.

"It's a shame this poison that's strangling our town," the preacher said to John. "You've lost half of yourself to it, son. Don't lose the rest. Join your mother at church one Sunday, you and Lucy are always welcome."

His mother and Sweetie were the last two left at the end of the visitation. People began to make lunch plans and quietly trickle out. Mamaw Perley had buzzed around for the entirety of the service, but Sweetie sat in the back alone and didn't even come to the front to see Anne. He only nodded when they made eye contact. When John looked up again, Sweetie had already left.

CHAPTER TWENTY-NINE

John and Lucy tried to go on with life the best they could after the funeral that day. Lucy played inside and John was changing the oil on the Oldsmobile when a state boy rolled up the driveway on him.

This trooper didn't drive the typical smokey gray Charger with the Kentucky State Police emblem shining on the side. John thought he had more of a detective look to him than your everyday jughead. He stepped down out of an unmarked SUV. The pretty-boy type, he had his hair fashioned in the front and wore a crisp, pressed polo shirt with the collar so stiff it dug into the man's neck. His khakis were pleated and had a crease down the center of each pant leg. His leather penny loafers got a little dirty as they stepped through the gravel toward John.

"Hey there! My name is Detective Phillips with the Kentucky State Police," he said. John wiped his oily forearms across his brow but didn't respond.

"Are you Mr. Perley?"

"I am."

"You have my condolences, John. Can I call you John? I'm sorry about your wife's passing."

"I'd prefer you didn't call me anything. What do you want with me?"

"As you know our officers recovered your wife's body and...well, quite frankly that's what I'm here to speak with you about, sir. I think you know where we found her and how we found her. I think you pretty well knew about your wife's death before our department ever did."

"I don't really care being told what I know and don't know," John said and spat into the yard.

"Then would you mind telling me for yourself then?" Phillips asked.

Oil dripped down John's fingertips. He realized he was still holding the old filter. He'd nearly forgotten all about the warm cylinder shape still hanging in his grip, but something about it made him feel more in control of the conversation. The dark liquid trickled from the filter's mouth and pooled on top of a flattened cardboard box before streaming into the gray dusty gravel between the two men.

"I ain't saying shit. You got enough gel in your hair to grease my ass and fuck me over as is, much less I go and start yakking my own jaw." John could feel his heart racing. "All I know was she'd been out running around with anybody who'd give her a pill, officer. God's honest truth."

"Look, John…"

"Don't call me John."

"I don't have to be the bad guy here. This doesn't have to come down on you. I know y'all got it from somebody right here around Turkeyfoot or else we wouldn't even be having this conversation. This whole community has been eaten up by these pills. We can't let this fentanyl come in on top of everything else. You can help us out here. This stuff is bad news, and you know it the same as I do."

"There ain't no community around here." John sat the oil filter at his feet and wiped his hands on his shirttail.

"Won't be for long if we keep up like this, Mr. Perley."

John stared down the road beyond Detective Phillips and could feel his throat clenched. He thought maybe this man with a badge was right. He thought about breaking down and giving the law everything they wanted. He could see it playing in his head while the state trooper stood firmly before him. He wanted to get down on his knees and confess everything that happened, drive this man with his pleated khakis straight over to Sweetie and they could all go to Tim Stevens' place right after that. He'd probably still do some time himself, but he could get help there. Lucy could stay with her mamaw, where she probably wanted to be anyways. He could feel it all at the tip of his tongue, but he choked it down and just stared through the officer to the road below.

"Mr. Perley, you ought to at least do what's right by

that little girl playing up there." Detective Phillips nodded towards the porch. John swung his head around to see Lucy had been watching and listening just like she always did.

"I'll take care of her just fine. You worry about yourself. Is there anything else I can help you with?"

"You ain't helping neither one of us very much today. Consider this talk a courtesy. I'll be back later with a warrant, and I'll be taking a look inside the home and the vehicle . I'd hate for social services to get dragged into all this."

"Come on back then. I'll be looking forward to it, mister."

John slammed the hood of the car down and turned back towards Lucy. He could feel Phillips watching him every step up those rickety stairs.

CHAPTER THIRTY

Sweetie couldn't believe nobody had asked too many questions about Anne. Or if they had, they hadn't connected him to it. The fact that he hadn't heard anything at all sat him on edge. Even if he didn't think it was his pill that killed her, he felt some responsibility for the Perleys. But it seemed not many were concerned with another young person overdosing in Eastern Kentucky.

Sweetie's house was silent. He could hear the kindling shift inside the wood furnace and the embers flared up. It wasn't cold out. The fall weather had mostly been fair, but the fire was at least something to tend to. The glow heated his face in the surrounding darkness of the living room. It was faint from where he sat on the sofa, but the warmth reached him.

The cuffs of Sweetie's pants rose above his ankles, he tapped his heel against the wooden floor. He still wore a rose lapel from Anne Perley's service that morning. There weren't any pallbearers, but friends and family were marked by the artificial flower. He doubted John had much to do with it so it disturbed him that somebody from the church had deemed him close enough to Anne to get special treatment. The needle poked through its green bound stem into the soft cloth of his jacket and every now and then he felt it brush against the skin of his chest like a reminder. Behind him, outside the window, there were clouds floating below the moonlight. They sailed weightlessly above the faint outline of the mountaintops. Broad swaths of black space separated them. Sweetie pulled the shade closed and kicked his dress shoes into the center of the room. He peeled his socks off and tossed them into balls at the end of the couch. When Sweetie had seen Lucy crying, everything felt like it funneled out of his chest until only emptiness remained. With his father gone to the nursing home to die, the small black living room of his parents' home was all that existed to him for the time being. He sat with his tailbone on the edge of his seat, his knees bent half below him as though he were about to stand up. Sweetie stared into the red door of the furnace, watching as it burned down to a dull glow.

Another piece of firewood fell inside, and the sparks flew out of the gritted teeth. Sweetie's mouth was flat as a nail against the rest of his face. His dark pupils fed on the stove's flames. His chest grew tight as he remembered his father's first day at the old folks' home. Sweetie could hardly stomach watching the man who raised him take a trip to the commode with a nurse holding his hand. The old Goodins man had fallen asleep while *Gunsmoke* played on a TV mounted to gray drywall. Sweetie had thought the old man's face looked sagged to one side. Half of his wrinkled cheeks, littered with liver spots and stray tufts of hair, looked like they would drip down onto the floor.

Sweetie wiped his face and felt a sting from the fire's heat. He took his phone from his pocket and flipped it open, its soft glow showing seven missed calls from John Perley. Sweetie tossed it down to the end of the couch with his dirty socks before rising from the sofa. He crossed towards the hall to his father's bedroom door and stood there for a moment. Sweetie twisted the knob, stepped inside, and reached for the light switch. The room was tight, a full-size mattress took up a corner while a dresser stood against the opposite wall. On top of the dresser, Sweetie eyed over some of his father's belongings. A tray full of coins and pocketknives sat in the center, behind it, on a small rack, hung old watches and some gold necklaces. He took a ring from the tray and slid it onto his middle finger. It was silver with a polished black stone as big as a knuckle.

Sweetie could hear his heartbeat against the inside of his sternum. The only sounds were himself and the wood stove. He fell onto his father's bed and drifted off to sleep, his head spinning like a top between his shoulders.

He dreamed of his father chopping firewood in the middle of a stand of trees. The old man was surrounded by the forest with no road, or signs, or trails back home. He just stacked split blocks into a pile against a broad tree trunk. Sweetie wanted to stop his father and split the wood for him, but he couldn't speak out. His words clung like phlegm in the back of his throat. The sun seemed to be dawning, and his father kept chopping. Sweetie reached out to lay a hand on the figure's shoulder, but he woke to the dimly lit room.

The wood he had added to the stove had really caught while he slept. He could feel the heat prickling his skin all the way back into his father's bedroom. Sweetie's eyes traced the wooden ceiling planks until they came to a knot in the log. He stared at the dark swirl against the otherwise straight-grained board then he sat up to see the clock. It was well past eleven.

Sweetie walked back into the living room and realized he never even locked the front door. He looked himself up and down in the mirror, still dressed in suit pants and a white button-up. He slid the pants off and dug around in a drawer for his usual jeans and a T-shirt. Sweetie stepped out on the front porch into the cool evening air. He stepped carefully across the wooden surface so that he wouldn't get a splinter in his bare feet. The wind was stiff but beginning to calm. Sweetie craned his neck towards the night sky. Most of the clouds had blown away. The stars spilled together and spread out again. He unzipped his pants and urinated over the edge of the porch step. His black Chevrolet sat parked nose end towards the house. His knees quivered some as he zipped his fly back up. He headed back inside and collapsed onto the couch with his legs spread wide and his head to the ceiling. Sweetie's mind fell back to Lucy and John Perley.

Poor girl, he thought. She was probably dirty and hungry if her grandmother hadn't come for her yet. John would snort them out of house and home without anyone there to stop him. More than likely, they didn't even have electricity or wouldn't soon. Sweetie had seen worse though. He had seen kids half naked in the winter, and the only thing keeping the place warm a kerosene heater running on fumes. Hungry, scared, hollow-eyed children. Sweetie wanted to save the girl somehow. But he knew he had done most of this to her. He had no small hand in saddling her young family with this evil. He had taken everything they had to their name and in exchange fed them rot and death.

He had destroyed her entire world beneath her living feet. She would grow up to be just like her mommy and daddy. Sweetie's stomach felt like a pit inside of him. He wanted to kneel and vomit, but he couldn't raise his head from the couch. The room turned around the man. The furnace had nearly burned down. Sweetie rubbed his eyes with the heel of his palms. His father's black stone ring glowed softly on his finger in what light remained. He pulled his phone from his pocket and stared at the missed calls from John again. Twelve now. Sweetie knew the boy must be sick from withdrawal. He thought of the bag of pills still stashed in the bed of his truck. There was at least a handful of Oxy and Percocet he needed to sell. Sweetie punched the callback button with his index finger and put the speaker to his ear. He listened as the young man's hoarse voice answered on the other line.

"Hey," John said. "You got anything?"

Sweetie didn't answer. He still lay leaned back against the couch, his arm bent holding the phone to his ear. The room was black now that the furnace had finished dying out.

"You there?" John asked.

Sweetie's lips tried to form the words he wanted to say but couldn't breathe any life into.

"I just need one or two. I have a nice chainsaw. It's about new. Husqvarna." John was getting chatty in anticipation of getting high. He was happy to stave off the sweats even if it meant peddling off some unfortunate soul's stolen chain saw. Sweetie thought of his dream, his father chopping firewood in the forest.

"Is it one of those junky battery-powered ones, or does it take gas?" Sweetie finally asked. He could feel John's chill break over the line at his response.

"Oh, it's gas," John snapped back. "Can you ride down here? Or I can hitch a ride up there. I'll be up there in a few. Don't go anywhere, Sweet."

Sweetie closed the phone and tossed it onto the end table. A picture of his parents on their wedding day faced him. They stood side by side smiling broadly, their elbows hooked with the steeple of the church behind them against a colorless sky.

Sweetie sat up and snatched the fire poker from its hook on the wall. He stoked the ash and added a few more logs to the metal box. He stuffed some crumpled newspaper in and slammed the door shut. He paced back and forth for a minute before turning the porch light on, stepping back outside and down to his truck. It was almost midnight, but Sweetie knew John would wrangle somebody to drive him out no matter how late. Sweetie pulled the bag out of his toolbox and quickly counted the pills off in his head. He pinched out a handful or so and stuffed the rest into his boot.

Back inside in the kitchen, he pulled the light switch and stood in its yellow glow for a moment before tossing the pills onto a small circular dining table in the corner. He and his father had always joked that it was more of a card table than anything. Sweetie turned to the coffeepot and began rinsing out what was left over from that morning, swirling hot water around in the glass carafe, dumping it down the drain. He refilled it with cold water and poured it into the back of the coffee maker. He grabbed a canister of Folgers from the cabinet above the stove and scooped a cup of grounds into a paper filter, tamping it into the top and pressing the start button. Sweetie went back to the running faucet and dipped his hands into the flow. He splashed his face and rubbed his eyes with his calloused fingertips. He ran his wet hands through his hair and swept it to one side then shut the water off. The house was silent again other than the coffeepot bubbling and hissing.

Sweetie couldn't help but feel odd having John come up in the middle of the night like this. He was used to being mindful when it came to someone coming to buy dope. Not that the old man didn't know what Sweetie did. Of course, he knew. His father wasn't a fool. That didn't mean Sweetie was going to blatantly disrespect him by doing it in plain sight. Sweetie took a coffee mug out of the cabinet and dipped some sugar out of a small glass dish. He dumped the sugar into his cup, poured the coffee over it, and stirred it a few times with a spoon. He watched the amber liquid spin and then he raised it to his lips to take a sip. Sweetie felt his stomach churn and the coffee dry out the back of his throat.

Just then Sweetie heard somebody pulling up to the front of the house. He sat the mug down and walked to the door to meet John. He looked out and could see the younger man talking and shuffling around inside the Estes boys' Astro van. The younger one sat in the back and Sweetie couldn't see him very well. Case, the older one, was driving. He couldn't be any more than twentysomething. He had scrawny arms from what Sweetie could see. His long, brown hair hung down loose, combed down straight at the sides of his face. Sweetie watched as John and the Estes hippie talked something over and finally John handed what looked to be a cigarette pack across to him. The passenger door opened and John stepped out wearing dirty sweatpants tucked into bright brown work boots. He had a Carhartt jacket zipped up tight with the hood pulled over his freshly shaved head.

"What do you know, man?" John asked in a chipper tone.

Sweetie watched as John swaggered to the back of the van and opened the back hatch up. John heaved and pulled out a bright orange chainsaw that shone under the moonlight. Case Estes shifted into reverse and turned back down the driveway. John grinned ear to ear as he stepped up across the yard and sat the machine on the edge of the porch by Sweetie's feet.

"What is this?" Sweetie asked.

"It's that chainsaw." John rubbed his hands together and then slapped his palms flat against his thighs.

Sweetie could feel his face flatten and he imagined himself grabbing John's lying tongue, reaching out and pinching it between his thumb and finger. The machine was rusted, more than likely locked up, and the bar looked warped so that it wouldn't cut straight even if someone got it running.

"This ain't no count for nothing. You came all the way up here after midnight to set this down on my porch?" Sweetie said.

John's smile had twisted into a set of pursed lips, and he looked like he wanted to smack Sweetie across his wrinkled face.

"Well, give me something for it, even a half of one at least," John swung his boot up to rest on the front step.

"I bet this thing wouldn't even cut straight. I'll wager you this, if you can get it started up and running, I'll give you a Percocet for it. It'll be worth that much just to cut up some firewood for the furnace."

John stepped up into the glow of the porch light and Sweetie pulled him a stool over to sit on. He fiddled with the choke for a second and then pumped the purge bulb with his thumb a couple times. John hauled back and yanked the cord, but the tired machine just coughed and died. He ripped it again but pulled the rope out the full length. The saw cackled as John fluttered his finger against the trigger. The blade spun around and around making a clicking noise like metal tapping on metal. When John took his finger off the gas, the machine idled. He sat it back down at Sweetie's feet with a smirk across his face.

"Now that's at least worth a thirty. Come on, Sweetie. That's a fine saw. You know it is. They don't make 'em better than Husqvarna."

Sweetie reached down and picked up the saw. He revved the engine up a few times and then killed it. He let it fall to his side holding it tight in the grip of his right hand and motioned for John to follow him into the house. Sweetie set the chain saw down in the front room, on the floor next to the furnace. He kept walking on back to the kitchen, picking up his coffee and sitting down at the card table. John followed closely and joined him. The older man handed him over a round tablet with an M stamped into it, an Oxycodone thirty milligram. John's eyes swelled some when he got more than he expected, but he didn't act as though anything was out of the ordinary.

"You got a plate or anything?" John asked.

Sweetie grabbed a saucer down from the cabinet and John greedily fell on the pill. Sweetie watched as the young man ground it down into a powder and used his driver's license to divvy it up into a couple of rows. John snatched a paper towel and blew his nose aggressively. He threw the napkin into the garbage can and sat back down at the saucer. He snorted the first and then the second without much of a pause in between, then pinched his nose tight and tilted his head back for a minute. John shook his head and reached for another paper towel. He stifled a cough and tilted his head back once more before blowing his nose into the napkin. Sweetie frowned as John set the bloody, snot-filled paper towel on the tabletop.

"Throw that in the damn trash can," Sweetie said. "Don't you have any shame?"

John could only nod. He took the napkin and folded it up in his hand and then sat still with his head down. Sweetie stood up and rinsed his coffee cup out in the sink.

"You want any coffee? Water?"

"Nn-no." John dragged on the front of the word with the loose tip of his tongue. Sweetie grabbed him a cup and filled it with tap water anyways. He placed it on the table next to the saucer. John stared at it with flattened eyes before rubbing his palms against his temples. He looked back up at Sweetie and smiled.

"You're one of the few good friends I got, Sweetie. You ain't never turned me down if you ain't had to."

"How you and Lucy been doing?"

"I think she took it pretty hard, but she's strong. She's

hardened up a lot. Doesn't talk as much. Mostly either stays in her room to herself or walks down to the creek."

"I'm sorry, John. I know it can't be easy on y'all."

"It was bound to happen sooner or later. I guess I just always hoped it'd be me first."

Sweetie didn't know what to say. He felt alone without his father at home, but he had never had a wife to lose.

"State boy come up to the house."

"What?" Sweetie's heart dropped.

"He was asking me questions about Anne." John rubbed the back of his hands against his eye sockets. "I could tell by the way he was talking he don't know shit."

"What was he saying?"

"He mostly wanted to know where the stuff she took come from. Don't worry though, I didn't tell him nothing. It wasn't you that killed her anyways, it was that damn fake dope from Tim Stevens. I should've flushed that shit, Sweetie. They towed the Olds. Said they were doing forensics or some bullshit."

"Has Tim said anything to you about it? Surely, he knows what happened," Sweetie said. But John had started to doze in and out. The young man's head lulled upon his neck like a half-deflated balloon.

Sweetie dried his coffee cup with a dishcloth. He set it in the cabinet, flipped it over on its rim, and then he walked past John to the front room of the house. He gripped a block of wood in one hand and opened the door to the furnace with the other. He stoked the ash inside enough to get it heated again and then threw in some wood chips to help it catch.

John's head lifted and his eyes scanned the room as though he was wondering where Sweetie had gone, but he wasn't all there. John folded his arms up and rested back against the wooden chair. Perfectly content in his present relief.

CHAPTER THIRTY-ONE

The next evening, Sweetie visited his father at the nursing home. The old man only woke up long enough to ask for some water and glare hatefully toward Sweetie for a few minutes. Sweetie sat and thought about growing up, he thought about sitting on the bottom step of the wooden porch with his legs kicked out. Resting while over the hillside storm clouds rolled over one another. Even with the promise of rain and a cool breeze, the sun was always stubborn. Sweetie's mother used to smile on hot days when all her boys came staggering up from the bottom where they always planted their crops. Sweetie remembered how they'd all hug her and she'd pour them up tall, yellow glasses of lemonade. The taste was sweet, but the thought of her lemonade left the roof of Sweetie's mouth dry now that he was no longer so young.

Sweat would drip from every crease of his teenage body. His jeans clinging to his thighs and each drop of sweat knocking a little more dust off his boots. Behind him would sit his mother and father, each in their own rocking chair at the top of the steps. His oldest brother, long dead now, squatted down in the yard, cutting a plug of tobacco. He always feared he'd end up having a hateful streak much like his older brother had back then. A watermelon would be dripping wet on an old coffee table the family had moved outside. The melon was always fresh and fat and untouched, saved just for those particular days. Sweetie's father would pack a wood pipe and take short, fast puffs. His younger brother, also dead now, leaned against the porch railing with ice clinking around in his glass. Sweetie's family had been good enough people. They had lived honestly in hard work. Even if they didn't get out to church all that often, at least their Bible had some creases in the spine and some tears in the pages. But there was a reason he always sat on the bottom step. Sweetie had plans to head to the biggest city he could back then, even if that was just the next town over. He was always watching that farm gate, and it was swinging wide open.

Sweetie didn't wait for his father to wake up before he left the nursing home. He figured the old man preferred it that way; it was easier to sulk and fester in anger alone. The lights in the lobby seemed dimmer on his way out. He noticed a new receptionist had started her shift.

"Take care of him for me," he joked with a smile on his way out, like he always did.

"I'll do my best!" she quipped back.

CHAPTER THIRTY-TWO

As he arrived at home, Sweetie's heart jumped into his throat. He noticed the front door of the house ajar. He pulled the front end of the truck up to the edge of the yard so that his headlights cast their light across the front of the house. The white siding was flat in the yellow glow. He flipped the high beams on and shifted the truck into park, but left the engine idling. The door stood motionless, cracked open just enough that a broad dark gap was all Sweetie could see. Both windows were hollow and dead, their curtains hung motionless. He leaned forward and felt under the seat for the old snake pistol, then opened the truck door, stepping out without shutting it.

The truck cab *dinged* and *dinged* behind him to let

him know the door was still open. His legs were wobbly as he stepped up the narrow, broken sidewalk towards the porch steps. The rest of his body was tense, his feet and knees tingled beneath him. Every one of his muscles was ready to jump out of his flesh at the slightest start. The man's ears filled with the sound of his own rushing blood. He couldn't hear someone inside if he wanted to, but he tried anyways. When he stepped up on the porch Sweetie pressed the metal barrel of the gun against the flaking white paint of the door. All at once he shoved it wide open and scanned the front room with his eyes leveled on the pistol's sights. Behind him, outside in the night, a bird whistled and took flight causing Sweetie to completely wheel around and aim the pistol back out the front door towards the truck. The headlights shone in his eyes, and he stood blinded in the doorway with his heart shaking and the truck's chime ringing in his head.

Sweetie focused back on the house. He pointed the barrel of the gun back towards his father's bedroom and slipped through the doorway. He flipped the light on and found the dresser tossed. His father's clothing and underwear lay piled on the bedroom floor. The tray of coins and knives, the watches and jewelry were all cleared out. The mattress was flipped up and the clothes in the closet had also been thrown onto the floor.

Sweetie stopped bothering to lock the front door. After the break-in, there wasn't much worth locking up anyways. Most nights when he returned home, he sat in the front room to watch the furnace burn until he went back to his father's bedroom and slept tirelessly. The fall weather had turned cooler. His dreams stopped for a time, but he had begun waking in the middle of the night to stand out on the porch. He would get up a few hours after midnight soaked in sweat. He craved the cold air on his bare chest and arms. He'd hope for the stars to be out and after a few minutes he'd turn and go back in where he would collapse onto the bed and not move until daylight.

Tonight, Sweetie tossed and turned. He kicked the quilt off himself and lay fixated on the ceiling. The mattress felt lumpy beneath him. His limbs were heavy, nearly impossible to lift, but he didn't even try, he just lay there awake and silent. He tried to will himself out of the bed, just to walk to the furnace to stoke it until the room glowed again. There were still a few blocks of firewood left and he knew the flames hadn't completely died down yet. Sweetie craned his neck forward and peered at the room around him. All he could see in the dark was the shape of the window cast across the room by moonlight, forming a cross on the wall next to him. The shape of the dresser was a black shadow against the silhouette.

Finally, Sweetie rose to sit at the edge of the bed. His steps were heavy as he made his way towards the furnace. He took the metal stoker from the corner of the living room and slung open the iron stove. Sweetie stabbed at charcoaled pieces of wood, half burnt and still smoldering. He stuffed another thick wad of newspaper into the square, metal mouth and piled three blocks of split firewood on top of that. When he closed the grated door again, he could see the flames start to lick at the edges of the paper and move up around the logs. Sweetie's body ached in the cold of the small house. The fire couldn't start burning soon enough to ease his shivering. He rubbed his hands together and stared into the mouth of the fiery pit.

CHAPTER THIRTY-THREE

John had started sitting on the porch way up into the night when he got high. Lucy liked all the different kinds of moths that flew down from the top of the mountain to sit with him. They twirled around the porch light while her daddy sat with his head hanging between his knees and drool running down his chin. By morning there'd be a flock of them clinging to the side of their house. As the sun cut through the fog, they'd start fluttering. Some were big as birds, their wings as wide as her daddy's calloused hands. Some wore splotches of lime green painted on their backs, a few looked like pink lemonade. Others were dark brown streaked with red up their sides.

Lucy was in her bedroom, but she wasn't sleeping just

yet. She was waiting for a moth to come down off the mountain. Lucy took her father's flashlight and shined it through her window into the backyard. She flipped it on and off until one just couldn't resist. They didn't always come, but sometimes she got one to land right on the window. Lucy looked at their underbellies. She wondered what they felt in their guts when they saw the light glowing, what made them float down from the poplars to look closer.

The moon was enormous above; it lit up smokey clouds that sidestepped across the sky. The only moth Lucy had seen that night was small and dusty. She didn't notice her father at first, but now the tip of his cigarette caught Lucy's eye. She cut the flashlight off and held her breath.

Her father sat at the edge of the back porch. He used to have great broad shoulders, but he'd become a wiry man especially since her mommy's funeral. Lucy could tell he had his medicine on his mind because he wouldn't stop shaking his knee. Up and down, he bounced his heel. He finished his cigarette and flicked it into the yard. He reached into his pocket and pulled out a wad of keys. The shed sat across the backyard from Lucy's bedroom window. The man crossed the grass, opened the door, and stepped in. The shadows consumed his figure, Lucy's eyes darted back and forth searching for an outline of the man. A light came on. Lucy still couldn't see him. A lonesome bulb swung above old boxes and scattered tools. She heard metal and wood scrape across the concrete floor. The night fell silent. The clouds had slipped off somewhere behind the mountains now. One of her father's electric saws whined to life inside the shed. The muffled sound of the blade ripped through Lucy's eardrums.

Lucy's room was gray and her eyes suddenly heavy. She didn't dare move from underneath her blanket. She breathed slowly. She listened to the clock on the wall and the blood pulsing through her ears. After some time, Lucy's bedroom door creaked open and she heard her Mamaw's voice.

"Lucy, honey. Mamaw's here. I need you to get some shoes on. Come on now, honey. Wake up."

Lucy flinched at the smoothness of her grandmother's voice, like cream pouring into the room.

"Your daddy had an accident, baby. Come on now, get ready."

Mamaw Perley's cheeks drooped over the corners of her mouth, just like her father's, and Lucy figured that one day hers would do the same. She climbed out of bed and slid into a pair of shoes without putting any socks on. She could feel her feet getting clammy and cold before she was even down the hallway.

When Lucy came around the corner, she was confused to see her father sitting upright and awake. He sat at the end of their musty, worn-out couch with a bloody rag wrapped around his left hand. A trail of blood ran from where he sat, dotting across the carpet and up to the brass doorknob. On the coffee table, resting on a fresh dishrag plain as day, was her father's pinky.

He didn't look at Lucy. His hand was bloody, but his face didn't show pain. He stared at the TV, but there was nothing on it. Just a black screen and his reflection. He bounced his leg and smoked another cigarette. His face was bony and his eyes were black.

Outside, in the dark of night, the hills were sleepy, and the air was cool. Lucy could tell that soon fall would give way to winter. Lucy's father slid into the passenger seat of her mamaw's SUV and Lucy buckled herself in the back. The seats felt slick and smelled fruity. Her grandmother climbed in and the vehicle hummed smoothly beneath the three of them. Lucy watched the streetlamps flicker by once they were in town. Cracks in the pavement *thump-thumped* beneath the car's wheels and red lights threw a glow in their faces each time the old woman stopped. John propped his hand on the middle console and stared down the hood of the car at the road. Lucy thought about the moths up high on the mountain in the tops of the poplar trees.

They pulled into the hospital lot, but Mamaw Perley didn't drive them straight up to the emergency room door. She parked with the other cars instead.

"You still have both your feet. You can walk," the old woman spat out at her son.

Lucy's daddy didn't respond.

Lucy stepped into the stale white light of the hospital. A doctor eyed her father up and down before paying any attention to his bloody hand. They took her father to the back and Mamaw started filling out paperwork. Her face looked like she wanted to cry and curse and pray altogether at once.

The bright lights in the emergency room gave Lucy a headache. The room buzzed, and she twisted around in her seat. She thought that a moth might like a place like a hospital, lit up and bright all over. Lucy rested her head in Mamaw's lap, her face turned away from the rest of the waiting room.

"You want a snack from the vending machine, honey?" Mamaw Perley nudged Lucy awake and began digging through her purse.

Lucy stared at the big leather purse with its brass zippers. The girl's eyes followed the floral patterns. Before she could answer, her grandmother was walking to the hallway where the vending machine sat. The old woman scanned row after row of junk food with pursed lips. A wrinkled dollar bill slipped from her billfold and she held it to the machine's mouth. The bill was spit back at Mamaw a time or two. Her cheeks were red and her mouth didn't close all the way. She took her heavy purse and slung it hard against the glass pane of the vending machine. Honey buns and sticks of gum rattled inside, but none fell.

Lucy woke up in her bed the next day and the room was bright. Sunshine rested silently on the toys that littered her floor. She climbed out of bed and looked out the window into the yard. The door to the shed swung freely on its hinges. There was a dark smear across the siding of the shed that Lucy had never seen before. She thought about her father's pinky on the coffee table. Lucy walked quietly down the hall and peeked into the living room. Her father was stretched out on the couch, but Marlboro Red smoke still hung in the air. The living room was clean and sunlight poured in from the windows.

The girl walked into the kitchen and pulled open the fridge. Inside there was a half-eaten jar of pickled bologna, a carton of eggs, and a jug of orange juice. She grabbed the orange juice and dragged a dining chair over to reach a cup. She took her drink to the living room and watched her father sleep, the man who used to twist his hips and sing *one for the money, two for the show* in the mornings seemed so far away.

His black hoodie was pulled down over his face. His left hand was wrapped tightly in fresh white bandages and his right hand clutched a bottle of pills. Her father must have been awake early this morning, probably even before any pharmacies had opened, nagging at her grandmother to go to town and fill the script from the doctor. Lucy watched for her father's breathing. She stood so still it felt like the world was running off without her. She closed her mouth tight and stared hard at his chest as it swelled up and fell again.

Mamaw opened the front door. The stocky woman huffed and puffed as she piled bags of groceries onto the kitchen table and then turned to switch on the coffee maker. Dark amber liquid began bubbling into the pot on the kitchen counter. She peered at her only son passed out on the couch. She shook her head and began filling the fridge with food.

"Put you on some clothes and get ready for church. Don't pay any mind to him, Lucy."

Lucy and her grandmother walked across the church parking lot. The off-white steeple was short and disappointing against the smothering gray sky above. Soggy hay bales lined a farmer's fence across the road. Lucy wondered where the farmer's cows were, but Mamaw pushed her along. There were cracks in the church-house steps up to the wooden double doors, and Lucy thought about tripping and falling into one of them.

Inside, the people at Mamaw's church looked glossy with sweat. Old men's guts stretched the seams of their stuffy collared shirts. The women had great big teeth and the stench of their hairspray made Lucy gag softly. Mamaw and her friends sat near the front, but Lucy hardly remembered the sermon.

Mamaw Perley's tears started on the drive home from church.

"Lucy."

She spoke her granddaughter's name and then her thin lips clapped tight. Lucy could tell she was holding back a whole wash of sobs.

"It wasn't always like this, honey. Do you remember that? You know you can stay with Mamaw as long as you need." The words dragged Lucy's heart down into her stomach like a lead sinker. Tears boiled over Mamaw Perley's hot face and down her droopy cheeks.

"I know, but I like it at home," Lucy answered.

"Your daddy isn't okay right now. It's not a place for a child."

"He needs me." The girl was glad when her grandmother didn't speak for the rest of the drive.

CHAPTER THIRTY-FOUR

The Perleys' trailer stayed dark most days after that. Even on autumn days with the sun high in the sky, her father had the shades pulled tight and all the lights out. John had been shaking his knee and staring at the blank TV all morning. He gagged and honked his nose as he snorted the last of his pills from the hospital trip. He pulled on his hoodie and cinched it so tight it swallowed his entire face. Lucy sat on the floor with a glass of her orange juice and played with toys while her father keeled over and began snoring on the couch.

A few moments passed. Lucy stood to take her father's hand into her own. She eyeballed the stub where his pinky used to be. The scab was rough and brown but almost healed now. It ran up the side of his hand like the saw didn't cut very cleanly. She stared at her father's hand and wondered how many fingers it would take to make him feel happy again. Not a word came from the pinched-up hoodie and his hand felt cool. The house was silent like in the winter when their kerosene heater would pop and kick off. As the winter came closer Lucy knew this would be her first Christmas without her mother. She could feel the single-wide trailer settling into the ground beneath them. Lucy's chest burned and tears blocked out her eyes. She took her cup of orange juice and threw it into her father's lap. The man's jeans soaked up the sticky, sweet liquid and Lucy's plastic cup fell to rest in the nook of his crotch. John didn't move, he slouched further over onto his side. Lucy thought about his bright-blue eyes on the mornings he'd sing and dance from one side of the living room to the other. The hands that once stretched down to scoop her up, now mangled forever.

CHAPTER THIRTY-FIVE

Sweetie Goodins parked catty-cornered at the end of the Perleys' driveway. The trailer rested on cinder blocks. Anne had planted two mulberry trees in the same hole on the east end of the trailer where the tongue hitch jutted out. Two scrawny trunks twisted together out of the ground and began to lean away from one another about a foot up. She planted them before Lucy was born. Each year they had bore their dark berries for Anne to admire before they grew overripe and fell to the ground in decay where the birds picked and clawed them to mush. The trees were bare now as the man walked up to the trailer in the cold. The front door was open, and Lucy swung her feet from the edge of the porch with a notebook and markers spread out by her side. She wore a windbreaker but had shorts on.

"Aren't you cold?" Sweetie asked.

"Not really."

"What you figuring on?" Sweetie pulled a peppermint from his shirt pocket and gave it to the girl.

"I'm drawing Turkeyfoot," she said.

"Drawing Turkeyfoot? The whole darn mountain?" Sweetie asked. "There's a whole lot of Turkeyfoot, how you going to map it all out from your front porch?"

The evening was brittle and silent. Sweetie could smell a crockpot of beans simmering inside. On the other side of the trailer, Sweetie heard John's saw running. The girl drew broad swooping green lines that Sweetie took as the mountains, and filled their shapes with bright red. Sweetie's eyes tightened on the strange choice of color.

"Where's your daddy?"

"He's in the back." The girl didn't look up from her picture.

Around back Sweetie found John at a sawhorse in front of his small shed. John was looking weathered. He wore oil-stained jeans and a Carhartt jacket covered in sawdust. Chunks of two-by-fours and planks littered the backyard. A picnic table stood between them. Its sharp corners and bright wood told Sweetie that John had just recently finished working on it and had already moved on to building something else. Sweetie ran his thumb along the splintered edge, mostly cut flush by the crude teeth of a SAWZALL blade.

John's veins stood up on the back of his hands. They

were full and green in the sunlight. Sawdust was stuck to his face and forearms. Sweetie would never get used to seeing the young man's four-fingered hand. It turned his stomach every time. John laid another piece of slabwood across the sawhorses. He held the plank firm with one hand, took his flat-nosed pencil and marked the cut with an arrow. The SAWZALL cut through the yellow poplar plank in one smooth motion. The smell of woodchips and coming rain sank thick in Sweetie's throat. Sweetie didn't know what to say to the man, as he stared at the nub where John's pinky used to be. Those off-yellow poplar planks buried the ground around John one by eight inches at a time.

"What are you doing back here?" Sweetie asked.

"Anne always wanted a picnic table out, so I finally made her one," John said.

"Well, it looks good. Didn't take you for much of a carpenter. Now what're you working on?"

"Don't know yet. Maybe a coffin." John stacked the newly cut plank neatly with a pile of others and laughed. "I'm just bullshitting. I'm aiming to patch up some of those sagging places on the front porch."

"That's good. You been doing alright? You staying sober?" Sweetie said.

"I ain't sober. I think about it every day. Can't not think about it. I'll never forget what it's like. The only thing I can do is try to stay busy."

"Well, I don't want to bother you. I'll let you get to it." Sweetie didn't have any more to say. It was him who didn't belong in this place. Sweetie turned to go, but before rounding the trailer he took one last look at John's hand as he carefully worked each tool. The younger man raised his face to meet his gaze and Sweetie would've sworn those blue eyes had welled up black for a second.

CHAPTER THIRTY-SIX

It still felt odd to John not making some kind of trade for a pill every time Sweetie came around. He was tempted every time but tried to remember what he had told the old man. He just had to stay busy. There was plenty to do; him and Anne had pretty much let the trailer fall into ruin while they spent all their time staying high. He was looking down into their septic line as he pinched his face up at the smell. When he had flushed the toilet earlier the water had kicked back and flooded the bathroom floor. Waste had built up and now flowed out the top of a lime-green PVC pipe. A white cap had fallen to the ground when he sawed it off. The tank was backed up somewhere down inside. He didn't have thousands of dollars to get someone to come out and fix it properly, so he took his drill bit and leveled it against the base where the pipe fed into the soft dark earth to the tank underneath.

His finger tightened against the trigger and the blade whirled its way through, the metal teeth spitting out shavings of plastic. It didn't take long for the force behind John's forearm to push through. Gray septic water drained out over his wrists before a half-digested chunk of hotdog clogged the hole. He picked it out with a stick and watched the rest of the sewage water flow freely down the hillside towards the ditch line.

The next day John Perley sat on the porch with a scowl across his face. A mean, pill-sick frown that made a man as likely to knock someone in the head as to say *howdy*. His jeans were muddy and stained with oil. Sweat ran down his face and chest, leaving shiny streaks in the grime that clung to his skin. Mamaw Perley's shiny new SUV purred as it rolled up in front of the porch.

"What the hell are you doing here? Leave, right now." John pointed his finger towards the road.

"Don't talk to your mother that way! I ain't going nowhere, where's my grandbaby?" She got out of the car but left the engine running.

"She's playing inside somewhere, get her and get out of my damn driveway."

"You're gonna have to tame that tongue before you can do anything with that nose of yours." Mamaw Perley rested her hands on her hips. She stared at her son's sunken cheeks and hollowed eyes.

Tim Stevens' F-150 truck turned in but stopped at the edge of the gravel as soon as it started up the hill.

"Who's that? Is that the scum that keeps you doped up? Is that who helped Anne kill herself?" Mamaw Perley threw her purse down on the hood of her vehicle and marched down the driveway towards Tim's truck, but it scratched backwards in the gravel and swung back around onto the main road. The old woman cursed into the darkening evening as the taillights rounded the curve and vanished. By the time she got back up to the hill, she was panting heavily. She marched straight past John and inside to get Lucy.

When she came back out with the girl, John thought about cursing and ranting and stirring up an argument because of her running Tim off. But he knew Lucy had already had plenty of that in her short lifetime.

"I'm thinking about going to rehab," he said.

"Well." Mamaw Perley turned to face her son. "That'd be good. Nobody else is going to do it for you." And then she left with Lucy.

CHAPTER THIRTY-SEVEN

John stood over the kitchen sink. The sun had just begun to rise. He bent down and splashed water into his face and mouth. A copperhead died at his toes; the head cut from the rest of its body. Its blood pooled on the kitchen tiles. As far he could figure, the snake had come inside seeking warmth as the colder weather took root. He wasn't the superstitious type, but the minute he saw it he had a bad feeling in his gut.

Lucy was staying with her grandmother while he got some things taken care of. Sweetie was driving him to Lexington that night to the cheapest rehabilitation center he was able to find. His mother had agreed to help with some of the cost if he was serious about it. He had to go today because he knew if he waited around, he would only end up backing out or overdosing.

He and Sweetie didn't say much on the drive up. He handed over what cash he had to help with gas and got out of the truck without another word.

That first night in rehab felt like wrestling a dragon. He twisted and turned in his sleep until he had thrown himself from his cot onto the ground. He fought to pin black wings to the cold floor, it flogged him until he cried, and its eyes shone red like a demon. His stomach tightened up inside of him, but it felt like his heart seeped out of his chest, under the door, down the hall, and into the center's parking lot where the sun dried it up and he finally found some rest. What little sleep he did get was filled with visions of Anne and years long gone. He hated those withdrawal dreams. It was almost always him and Anne when they were younger. Sometimes something to do with Lucy. His first night he had dreamed of a black snake.

People he knew always liked black snakes, said they were harmless and supposed to keep the real serpents at bay. In his dream the black snake wasn't harmless. It never slithered to the other side of the fence. It always turned to face him. He would draw a pistol to shoot. One of those big Colt Navy revolvers like cowboys in the movies carried. But the cylinder always crumbled, and the polished wooden grips came loose. The black snake would bite into the toe of his work boot and then it would unhinge its jaw, slowly working its way up his entire being until he couldn't breathe any longer. He could only cry. He always cried in the dream. A shallow whimper as he tasted his last bit of air and awoke to reality.

John laid in bed most of the morning after his night of memories and terrors. At lunch he trudged down the hall with everyone else to the cafeteria where he sipped grape juice from a plastic cup, the aluminum-foil top folded back neatly. He thought about leaving, he thought about calling Tim and getting high. He was too ashamed to tell Sweetie he'd already given up. The room was lit up with long rectangular lights that tried to sanitize all who inhabited the place. Plexiglas windows and steel double doors stood between him and a ride home, but all it would take was some paperwork and signatures.

When John finally walked out the front doors, the bright sun felt warm on his skin even though it was still December. He rubbed his eyes and sat on a bench. Tree branches came together in a broken canopy above him. A stone-faced statue of an angel prayed over a small koi pond. A breeze swiped across the barren parking lot. He closed his eyes and joined the angel in her prayer while he waited for Tim to pick him up.

CHAPTER THIRTY-EIGHT

It was about noon when Tim's F-150 pulled up. The wheels, the windows, and the grill were all blacked out like something John imagined a rapper would drive. The back end seemed squatted a bit and when John opened the door to hop in, he noticed the back was loaded down with bags of mulch.

Tim's bottom lip bulged, packed tight with two pouches of dip. He spat a long string of amber out the window while they drove down the interstate. The wind screamed into the open window.

"Nasty habit, I know," Tim said as he held the button and the automatic window climbed back up. "I just never could shake my appreciation for the tobacco plant. It's a part of our heritage."

John stared out at the fields as they passed by and thought about that first night in rehab, the black snake gobbling him up and dragon wings beating against his face. He found it hard to believe that it could have all been for nothing.

CHAPTER THIRTY-NINE

Mamaw Perley didn't say anything about the truck parked in the driveway when she let Lucy out by the porch steps. When the girl looked to wave, her grandmother was already turned around and pulling out on the road back towards town. Lucy slung her backpack up on one shoulder, it was stuffed full of new clothes and some snacks Mamaw had sent home with her. The kitchen light was on inside. Lucy looked for the moon above—the trees stood out against the gray night sky, and low-hanging clouds were illuminated in the moonlight. She took the first step up and glanced again at the yellow kitchen window, her heart filled with the presence of another person inside. She imagined just for a second her mother and father back at the kitchen table. Next thing she knew she'd quickened her pace and bounced over the last step to reach for the door. She scanned the half-lit living room for her father. The room smelled musty and wet, like a mongrel had been rolling around on the carpet. Lucy turned her eyes to the kitchen where the only light came from, still expecting her mother to be back from the dead, only to see a man at their dinner table. He wore a brown and tan flannel with the sleeves buttoned at his wrists. His appearance was neat, his shirttail tucked into a pair of ironed cream slacks, a wide leather belt with a brass buckle clasped tight. The man gave no indication that Lucy's arrival was anything but ordinary to him. He glanced at her and then at her father's slumped figure on the couch. He looked back to the girl and smiled. Lucy stood sure-footed and stared back. She refused to speak first, and she was determined not to return his smile.

"I'm Mr. Stevens, your dad's boss," he said.

"I know who you are." Lucy's small chest heated with anger at how softly his words floated across the room. She didn't know how she knew. But he was different from the others. The girl stared at the man at her kitchen table. His amber-colored eyes caught the kitchen light like a flame.

"You killed my mommy," Lucy said. The fire in his eyes vanished like two pits had formed in his head.

"Watch your mouth, girl."

"You gave us that bad stuff that killed her."

"Is this how two pillheads raise their daughter to speak to company?"

"You ain't no company to me!" Lucy squeezed the

strap of her backpack and stormed through the hallway to her room. She locked the door and sat with her back to it even though she knew if someone wanted in, she wouldn't be able to stop them.

CHAPTER FORTY

John didn't want to face Sweetie if he didn't have to. He didn't have any choice but to turn to Tim's fentanyl for the time being. The deal was he'd peddle them to his buddies, but he had no intentions of doing so. He let Tim front him some to get started and then hoarded it. He could feel something within himself going over the edge. He didn't want Lucy to be the one to find him dead if it happened. Lucy was better off at her mamaw's. After his mother had picked the girl up he hitched a ride straight over to the Estes' house so that he could at least have some company. He wasn't ignorant; he knew Anne and Case had a thing going on the side before her death. But all John wanted was to be around others who knew what it was like to be so sick you could hardly stand the light of day. He'd been there for a few days now. He felt the frame of their broken-down couch as he lay on his back staring at the ceiling, listening for anybody else who might be awake.

He liked staying uptown for a few reasons, like the Shell Mart and the Dollar General were a short walk, plus there was always plenty to get into, whether it was dope or making a little money. The Estes brothers lived in an old brick house their parents had left them. It was within earshot of the rail yard, and even though trains were sparse nowadays you could still catch the sound of one ever so often coming through the night.

Case Estes, the oldest of the two brothers, had a van that ran fair enough. It was an early '90s model Chevrolet Astro. Its bulky box frame carried an authority even if it was the ugliest sight on wheels John had ever seen. John had watched as Case once walked a brand-spanking-new set of tires right out of the sliding door at Walmart. He helped pile the tires into the old van and then they all turned out onto the bypass like any other customer that day. Case had pillheads all over the county trying their luck. Walmart, Lowes, or whatever someone had around. Some drove plum up the interstate to try their luck lifting from the Target. John had heard a story about the sheriff pulling up on one poor boy trying to steal out with a new stove on a hand dolly. They asked him where he lived and he told them all the way out at Blue Lick.

Case might have been crazy as a loon, but he did have that van, which was more than most junkies like themselves had to show. John didn't expect to see the

Oldsmobile back from the Kentucky State Police anytime soon. From what John could tell the Astro was a smooth ride—more than a few times in the past Case had let him borrow it to run up the mountain to pick up a couple of pills from Sweetie. When someone saw Case pull up in the brute, they just about knew he had a big idea brewing. They had all kinds of ways to make some money in a van like that.

John didn't have much of the synthetic dope left. He didn't want the two brothers knowing anything about it. Once he was sure he was the only one awake, he snuck out to the back porch and left Case and James inside asleep. John already knew it didn't take much to knock a body dead. The Esteses would kill themselves in no time if they started in on it.

He tied off his left arm with a leather belt. The metal buckle felt cold against his skin, the edge of the leather digging into the soft inside of his elbow just below his bicep. His rig had bent slightly, and the needle was becoming dull so he knew it would be hell finding a good solid vein. John imagined look-alike pills being made in a lab as he crushed one up. Probably down in Mexico or over in China on the other side of the world. He wondered if they ever sampled their own product. He hadn't mentioned anything else to Sweetie about the stuff. The old man would piss himself if he found out John had been going straight to Tim. Sweetie wouldn't want to be cut out like that.

John's bag was just about out though. He had a few dirty cotton balls he could probably get a wash out of later if he needed, but all that would do was keep him from getting sick right away. There was money to be had somewhere around Turkeyfoot. There always was. Whether it was waiting to be plucked up around the back of someone's shed or whether it was a matter of someone hatching a scheme to get in on. There was always something to do that would get them just enough to catch a buzz for the evening.

What he knew for sure was that he and Case would go out rogueing in the Astro, he knew the Estes boys would be feeling just as down as he was, and they didn't even have a secret stash that he knew of. The three of them could easily load the back of the van up with some power tools or scrap metal. Just enough to get a pill each was all they'd need for the day.

Back inside John dozed off on the futon. When he came to it was almost noon and Case was up stirring in the kitchen. When he walked in, Case was standing atop a kitchen chair cursing and slamming pots and pans together while rummaging through a cabinet. He wore a baggy hoodie with illegible silver writing across the chest—the print was jagged and sharp and smashed together, it looked like a heavy metal band's logo but some of the vinyl was faded and peeling off. His jeans were dirty and worn thin, the cuffs tattered around his ankles. He was tall and scrawny with long brown hair that he sometimes combed down straight, but most of the time it was a shaggy mess.

"We need to find some way to make a dime today," Case said with his back to John. "I think I got something for us."

"As long as it don't end with us locked up at Three Forks, I'm game." John leaned against the doorframe of the kitchen and watched as Case moved to the next cabinet and continued to dig, this time through dusty outdated appliances and empty mason jars. He thought about his stash and figured maybe Case did have something put back for hard times.

"What you looking for?" John asked.

"These." Case pulled a wad of crumpled burlap sacks out of the back of the cabinet, a tea kettle snagged them on the way out and tumbled onto the kitchen floor. Case didn't even bother to return the chair to its place at the dinner table. He hopped down onto both feet and tossed John one of the brown sacks.

"James! Wake your ass up!" Case shouted. He made his way to the back of the hallway and took his fist against his brother's bedroom door. John watched as Case snatched a pair of work boots from the back-door floor mat. Case leaned against the wall and pulled each boot over a bony foot. The leather of one was worn down so much that the steel toe was showing through.

"What are you aiming to do?" John asked.

"Walnuts."

"Walnuts?"

"A lot of 'em."

"Are those even in season?"

"They ought to be falling right about now. James! Get up or we're leaving you!"

"Fuck you!" James' muffled voice came from behind the flimsy bedroom door. John grabbed up his sneakers and sat down on the couch to pull them on. The bedroom door jerked open and James emerged from his bedroom in the same clothes he had worn the past few days: a tie-dye hoodie and a pair of khaki cargo shorts he was constantly pulling up because they were two sizes too big. John ran his hands through his hair and followed the two brothers outside, down the front steps to the driveway, and into the van.

CHAPTER FORTY-ONE

The Astro had the back row of seats ripped out a long time ago. John figured Case needed more room for his thieving and walnut harvesting. At least they could say today's work was honest enough though. Case claimed to know an old farmer down by the river who always offered up a crisp hundred-dollar bill for a full load of black walnuts. Between the three of them, a hundred bucks would be just about enough for a pill a piece and maybe even a cold drink from the gas station if they were lucky.

John sat in the back with his legs straddling a plastic tote. The Astro van thumped over a bridge as Case talked.

"This lady up here has a whole yard full of them. Her husband died off and now she ain't got nobody to clean up the front lawn for her. It's got to be about an acre or two all said and done. I swear there's a big row of fat walnut trees standing along her driveway. I'll head up to talk to her about what we're aiming to do, you two go ahead and start scooping, there should be some cardboard boxes in the back there with you, John. Use that plastic tote too, fill that bitch up to the brim."

Case was in rare form. He was not usually so chatty, so authoritative.

But John didn't care. He could tolerate a lot if it meant scoring. Once they were all loaded up, he would ring Sweetie and they'd ride up Turkeyfoot to the ridge. He'd been avoiding it for as long as he could, but now that he'd stiffed Tim it was back to relying on the old man from the mountain.

At the widow's house, John wore a thick pair of yellow, leather gloves that Case had in the van. The insides were like suede; he could feel the soft interior as he reached down and scooped up an armload of walnuts. The gloves' fingertips were stained black. John wiped the sweat off his brow with his forearm, trying not to smear their sticky grime onto his face.

"This shit is so nasty," James said.

"How would you know? All you've done is bitch, but I ain't seen you load half of what John and me have." Case cocked a fistful of walnuts back and pelted his younger brother in the back with them like a shotgun blast. "Lazy motherfucker!"

"Grow up, man. We ain't kids anymore. Do some shit like that again and I'm gonna hold you down and shove one down your throat." James plopped down at the base of a walnut tree and pulled his left boot off a pale, clammy foot with no sock.

"You ain't gonna do shit, fat boy," Case got down on his knees and used the hem of his shirt like a basket, "except sit there on your ass."

"I ain't even fat anymore, shut the fuck up. We ain't kids." James finished picking his toes and pulled his boot back on. John reached down and scooped up two more palmfuls before halfheartedly dropping them into the cardboard box he kept kicking around in circles. They had worked most of the trees but had slowed down now that the Estes were arguing and carrying on. John was starting to have doubts about the whole enterprise.

"Come on, y'all, let's finish this up so we can get paid," John said. He moved on up to the next tree to put some distance between himself and the bickering brothers. Case was cursing and yelling and kicked his brother's box over so that it spilled into a big mound of dark green and black.

By the time they heaved the last box full up into the minivan's sliding side door, everyone was feeling easier. The brothers were cutting up with each other as opposed to lashing out.

"Look what you've done, man," James said with a grin. "My nuts are all bruised up."

"You wish your nuts were that big." Case took a pair of

walnuts and held them in his hand like he was getting a sense of their weight.

John pulled his gloves off and rubbed his knuckles against his closed eyes. He pressed firmly against his eye sockets until he could see colored spots speckling against the back of his eyelids then he walked a ways off and took a piss on a chicory flower at the edge of the driveway. He never wanted to see another walnut; all he could think about was sinking a needle into his arm.

CHAPTER FORTY-TWO

John was beside himself when Case unloaded the boxes and the farmer counted out their money. He had been skeptical of the whole scheme from the minute he heard it. Their moods had been lifted by the time they pulled up into Sweetie's driveway. They could see him sitting on the front porch with a pocketknife in his hands. John got out to do the talking.

"You ain't got three of those green ones, do you?"

"All you fine young men. And every one of you is determined to let these little pills kill you. No bigger than the tip of your pinky and you'd trade the world for one."

"What good would it do us to live up and be an old man like you? What kind of an end is that?" John always hated when Sweetie tried to lecture at them. He couldn't see what moral high ground the old man had to stand on. "We ain't got much hope either way, the way I see it. Might as well catch a little buzz," John said.

Sweetie cleaned gunk from underneath his fingernails with the blade. His eyes were trained on his own hands. The sharpened edge of the knife was shiny compared to the rest of the age-blackened steel.

"Never know," Sweetie finally said. "If you're like me, you might stick around and figure out what a fool you've been."

"Come on, Sweetie. We got the money, stop bullshitting."

As soon as the Astro was bouncing down the old man's gravel driveway, they were looking for a place to shoot up. They drove back down off the mountain and parked at the closest Dollar General.

Case's fingers were still stained from the morning's toil. He had refused to wear any gloves, said they'd just slow him down. John watched as the black fingertips pinched one of the pills from the baggy Sweetie had given them, then handed the last one to James in the back. John had already ground his Percocet up with the butt end of a lighter into a silver spoon. The Dollar General parking lot was always a perfect place because John liked to go in once he was feeling easy and buy a snack. He usually came back out with a couple of energy drinks, Beast or Crank or whatever was stocked at the time. He liked the apple-flavored ones in the big fat cans. Sometimes he'd buy a stick of beef jerky if he had the money, but usually he didn't eat much at all.

John tied his arm off at the bend in his elbow. After cooking it for a bit he pulled the mixture of dope and water into his syringe and carefully rested it on the dashboard of the van. John poked at the crook of his elbow with his index finger. He prodded his two biggest veins and once he was satisfied that he could hit one, he took up the syringe. He was more careful with a loaded needle than anything in life, he didn't want to waste a drop of that priceless liquid. John stuck the fine point lightly against his chosen vein and then pierced it through his skin. Before shooting he pulled back a bit on the plunger until he saw his blood flush up into the mixture. James always swore you got a bigger hit that way, but John only did it to make certain he was in a vein.

He slowly pressed the plunger until every drop he could see had gone through. He gave it a jiggle before pulling it out like a cheap skate might rattle the nozzle of a gas pump into his tank. John's mind snapped together, he felt like he could breathe again. A chill immediately broke over him and sweat beads began to dry against his clammy skin. He nodded back in the front seat of the van for a minute with his eyes rolling inside his skull. After a moment of ecstasy, he snapped back up and looked across at Case with half-cocked eyelids.

"I'm gonna go in here for something." John's words melted over his tongue. The passenger door of the van squeaked as he popped it open. He paused to gather himself before stepping out, then confidently hopped down and strode across the parking lot, rubbing his hands against the back of his pants the whole way.

Inside the store, John stood, lazily scanning a giant bin of candies. He picked up a bag of sour gummies, the plastic package crinkling in his grip. He sat it back down. The entrance bell chimed, and John's glossed-over eyes rose to see a man in a pair of creased gray pants, a gun belt, and a gleaming gold shield hanging from a patch of leather. The man had a buzzed head, a freshly shaved box chin, and a big jug hat with the Kentucky State Trooper emblem pinned to it. A golden cord wrapped around the base of its crown and came together in two short tassels at the front. Him and John locked eyes only for a moment before John broke his gaze and turned to open a small cooler full of energy drinks and pop cans.

He thought he could feel the trooper lingering behind him at the door and knew he would have to face him. John tried to straighten his eyes in his head. The thought of Case and James in the parking lot came to mind.

The officer stood like a post between the doors and the only cash register with an employee. John knew he couldn't ditch the drink now without appearing even more suspicious. He squeezed the cold aluminum in his palm and wheeled around to head up to the counter. He trained his eyes on the ground, the conveyor belt, and then the woman with the black-and-yellow polo shirt. He could feel the officer looking him up and down. John focused on not letting his hands shake as he pulled a sweaty five-dollar bill from his pants pocket.

"I just got off my shift. I ain't trying to bother you any, buddy," the officer said. "Here."

John's heart thumped behind his sternum; he still couldn't fully look on the trooper's face. He raised his eyes enough to see that the man was holding a square slip of paper. A pamphlet. A dismantled set of shackles printed against a glossy white background with one simple sentence beneath the image: TIRED OF BEING A SLAVE? Inside there was a schedule of AA and NA meetings, phone numbers, information, and resources listed at a local church.

"Appreciate it, sir," John said. He couldn't believe the cop had come up to him like that. Just as quick as it had happened the man turned and left.

John folded the pamphlet and stuffed it into his shirt pocket. He paid the cashier and pushed through the door to the parking lot without waiting for any change.

CHAPTER FORTY-THREE

Hustling to stay high never stopped.

The next day they parked the box van on the lawn-and-garden side of the Walmart lot. Case and James sat up front watching old folk shuffle in and out of the sliding doors. It was a weekday, so the place was nearly empty. Most of the cars that pulled in were retirees and stay-at-home moms. John picked at a sore on the center of his palm in the back seat. Case was about a full knuckle deep in his nose, working on the second one.

"I ain't going in, I did it last time," James protested, digging at his crotch. "They might recognize me and then there we'd be."

"You mean there you'd be." Case moved his hand

suspiciously from his nose down to the edge of the Astro van's cloth seat.

"Well, I ain't going in," James repeated.

"Look at this son of a bitch." John pointed towards a brand-new, chrome-trimmed F-150 driving up the parking lot from the far end. The sun glistened off its waxed paint and shining black wheels. The truck swung wide as it nosed its way into a spot and Tim Stevens stepped out. He looked back at the new truck as he walked to enter the store.

"He sure is shitting in high grass, ain't he?" Case mumbled.

"Shoot, I'd like to open that big brute up and let it moan out of here." James' voice was giddy like a little boy. "I bet he's got the leather seats and all in there."

They bickered for a while longer and watched Tim leave. Case ended up going in. He was inside the store for what John reckoned had to be the longest 15 minutes in his life, then just when him and James were getting antsy, they saw him come through the automatic doors pushing a shopping cart with a pile of socket sets and hand tools in it. John held his breath as Case calmly strolled out before picking up his pace without gaining anyone's attention. John and James hopped out and opened the back hatch to the van as the three of them started pitching everything in. Case seemed cool—it was just a fact of his life at this point. He even took the time to push the shopping buggy over to its return corral. Besides, it wasn't even one of those big licks that local lore was made of. Just enough to get what they needed; Walmart could afford it. Case and James sold most of the tools off to a few of their father's old friends and stashed the rest at their house to sell later when they could. John offered to call up Sweetie, but the brothers had another plug they wanted to hit up this time around.

CHAPTER FORTY-FOUR

The Hardee's drive-thru stretched around the sandstone corner of the building, past the dumpster, and straight through the dirty parking lot. Right up to where Case's Astro sat, its fat square behind still hanging partially out in the main road.

"Are we seriously sitting here waiting to take this fat slob a thick burger?" John asked, digging at his fingernails with a yellow-handled sodbuster. It was his only pocketknife he hadn't sold for dope. His grandfather had given it to him. He dug the curved point of the blade just under the edge of a swollen red scab on his hand and pried up until the piece of skin came loose.

"I already told you that's Bubby's deal! If you bring him

a combo, he'll throw you one of them Xanax bars in, no charge. Shit, I ain't too good for that." Case laughed and edged the van a little bit forward in the drive-thru line.

"I don't like them damn bars no ways. Turns everyone into a rogue. Blacking out and going crazy." John snapped his mouth shut after he spoke.

"Well, like 'em or not, Bubby owes James and me one." Case grinned—John caught a glimpse of his stained, chipped teeth. "And we aim on getting what's ours."

Bubby was the only junkie John had ever met who hadn't been worn down to nothing but skin and bone. He was always careful to make sure he came out on top when he got into a trade with someone. Ever since he started running pills, he stayed armed to the teeth with new pistols and rifles. John thought that was fair enough. Given his clientele, there was good reason for his paranoia.

When they finally got to the intercom, Case ordered a frisco melt with curly fries and a large Mello Yello. Bubby lived uptown too, but he was farther down on the east side where the train tracks and the river bumped up against one another.

When they walked into Bubby's, the first thing John noticed was the man's belly hanging out of the bottom of his holy T-shirt. His legs were covered with stained sweatpants. His swollen shins stretched the soft cotton pant legs. Case tossed the food in front of where he sat on a couch, onto a coffee table cluttered with mail, empty pop cans, different remote controls, and a matte black Glock. Leaned up against the couch next to Bubby was an AR-15 with a tiny scope mounted atop it.

"What y'all up to, Case?" Bubby said as he took up the brown bag and looked inside at his meal.

"Just trying to get by, looking for a little something. You good?"

"Shit, man. You know I'm always stocked up." He unfolded the frisco from its paper and squeezed it between his pudgy fingers. "Whatever y'all need I got it."

Bubby wasted no time biting into the burger. Mayonnaise dripped down into his wiry neckbeard and he smeared it away with the back of his hand. In what seemed like no time he'd polished off the carton of curly fries and worked his way down to the last few bites of the sandwich. He wadded up the burger's wrapping paper and stuffed it into the empty fry carton before stuffing that into the empty brown paper bag. His breath was somewhat labored as he reached down and drug a wooden box from under the coffee table. He opened the lid and his puffy fingers plucked up two little white bars with thin grooves striped down the length of them so that they could be broken up into sections.

"There's that for ya." He handed one to Case, who quickly stuffed it down his shirt pocket. Bubby crushed the other with the butt end of the black pistol and then snorted it off a small saucer with inlaid sunflowers lining the rim.

He repeated the entire motion again and snorted another one of the Xanax, cackling and hacking up phlegm until his whole body shook.

"Woo-wee! Somebody call the law." The round-faced man coughed so hard his face turned bright red. "Tell 'em come and get me! I'm running wild, boys!" He began banging the stock of the long rifle against the floorboards between his legs. John thought he saw Case and James exchange a glance, but he couldn't look away from Bubby. The man's flushed red cheeks were pocked in several places with what looked like acne scars.

Before John realized what was going on, Bubby slung the rifle up and pulled it tight to his shoulder. He fired three rounds off through the front wall of the house, right past where John and the two brothers stood. John's ears rang and the smell of gunpowder burned his nostrils. Drywall lay crumbled in a pile on the floor at the other end of the room, smoke coiled out of the rifle barrel, and beams of light shone through the newly formed bullet holes right on Bubby's stomach. John thought his eardrums had to be busted, he couldn't hear anything but ringing. It felt like a dreamy daze as he saw Case scramble around the coffee table and pin the rifle against Bubby's gut. Case struggled to hold Bubby down and control the rifle. On the other side, James snatched the pistol and started bringing its metal frame down across Bubby's face. The first time it just sounded like a flat thud. John saw blood trickle down when the second strike landed. By the third, James had hammered Bubby's face in pretty good and the large man was spitting teeth and his nose looked squished over to the side in an L shape.

John's mind was blank, but his body was trembling with adrenaline. Before he even knew what he was doing, he had snatched up the wooden pillbox and was screaming at the Estes brothers to come on. Case pointed the rifle at Bubby's chest and kicked the coffee table over. James wiped blood off his hands onto the back of his cargo shorts and stuck the pistol into his hoodie pocket. Bubby laid over on the couch holding his face in his hands, whimpering and gasping out sharp wheezing noises.

"Why'd y'all go and do that for?!" Bubby cried out.

"What all's in there, John? Open it up!" Case said, panting slightly, trying to catch his breath from the struggle.

"Y'all somebody's bound to have called the law after he took off shooting like that. Let's get the hell out of here." John was at the door with the wooden box cradled under one arm. He peered out the front door window blinds, but the street outside seemed calm and quiet. He could feel his stomach turning and his ears pricking up to listen for sirens.

"Give me that!" James pulled the box out of his grip. Case backed towards the door to leave but kept the rifle trained on Bubby. The man blubbered incoherently and then the three of them were out the door and gone as though they never came.

CHAPTER FORTY-FIVE

Other than the occasional run to the gas station for cigarettes or food, they mostly holed up at the brothers' house. There hadn't been much cash in Bubby's little box, but there were a lot of different pills and that was better than any currency in their eyes. Staying high and not having to worry about how they were going to scrounge something together was nice. But like always, the dope ran out.

Case stayed blasted out of his mind on the Xanax and with what cash there had been he kept buying liquor, so he was a fit to be tied just about every night. The wooden box had run pretty much empty one night when Case and James came to blows over an allegedly missing Oxy thirty milligram. John knew with the way they'd all been having at it there was no telling which one of them had shot it up. James initially got the better of his older brother, but Case wouldn't let it rest and ended up sucker punching James in the back of the head after the younger brother had turned his back. John tried to break it up and took a lick or two for his trouble. Before things got too ugly he figured it was well past time to head back home for a spell and lay low on the mountain. He didn't want to be around if Bubby came to visit anyways, so he took off walking towards the gas station with hopes of bumming a ride from Sweetie.

For the most part, John tried not to think about how much he owed Sweetie. There was no way to put a hard figure on it—he had lost track of any notion toward a specific amount a long time ago. He simply knew he could never pay it all back. In some way it had lost any meaning and so he continued to take like a leech with two legs. There had been a time when he felt guilt and shame burning in his chest whenever he spoke to the older man. But over time such shame waned to numbness.

In recent months that numbness had begun to feel like hatred. He hated the man he would have previously called a friend. There was times John had told Sweetie he would rather be dead than laid up sick from withdrawal. Sweetie would always come around just in time to help him feel better and get him feeling good again. The hatred made him wish Sweetie would've just let him go. Anything to cease the endless toil of feeding this pit in his heart and soul.

John was waiting now for Sweetie to pick him up at

the edge of town, outside of the newly built Circle K, drinking soda from a Polar Pop cup. The large neon sign glowed bright red and white above him as he sat on a curb, staring out across the freshly paved blacktop, watching an old woman fill her SUV with gas. He imagined she'd be the type to pay extra for the premium fuel, as the vehicle still had dealer tags hanging on the back of it, and a corner piece of the baby-blue paper flapped in the breeze. John sucked his sugary fountain drink down until only the ice rattled inside and then took the lid off the top and bit a hunk out of the foam cup's rim. He spat it out onto the ground and bit another piece off, chewing on it slowly between his front teeth. The woman at the gas pump loaded back into her new SUV and pulled out onto the main road. He spat again and tossed his empty cup into the gas station's dumpster.

The night air was cool, but John was feeling numb otherwise. He had just finished shooting up with Case and James a few hours before the fighting broke out, but knew Sweetie wouldn't give him a ride if he had been over at their house. Sweetie had never cared for the two brothers and by now he had probably caught wind of what happened to Bubby. John's mouth was dry, and his head was freshly buzzed courtesy of an old pair of clippers he'd found under the sink in James' bathroom. He had just enough minutes left on his prepaid cell phone to call Sweetie and ask for a lift back to the mountain. It was later than the old man liked to get out, but not so late that he'd turn down the prospect of selling a couple of Oxy.

Two beaming yellow headlights cut across the lot and

fell upon John where he sat with his legs crossed beneath him. He held a hand up to shield his eyes and squinted as Sweetie's black truck slowly rolled up beside him and came to a stop where it idled. The tinted windows were impossible to see through in the dark, but John knew the older man sat inside with a scowl across his face waiting for him to get up and hop in. John stood, a little unsteady on his legs but he put one in front of the other confidently and crossed the front of the truck straight through the bright lights. He yanked the truck's door handle, stepped on the running board, and climbed up into the seat.

"Thanks for getting me," John tried to sound casual, but he could tell Sweetie wasn't in any mood to chitchat. "I didn't want to get hit by a carful of drunks walking all the way up the mountain."

John settled into the cloth seat and pondered on whether he should keep a conversation on life support the whole drive or just let it be and shut up. He had always found it hard to just shut up.

"What you been up to on this beautiful evening, Sweet?"

"Working," Sweetie said. John turned his gaze out the window where a herd of cattle grazed in a pasture, enjoying the nighttime breeze.

"How's your old man been doing?"

"He's seen better days, but he's good I reckon. Just hates that old folks' home they got him in."

Sweetie didn't offer any more than that and John wished he hadn't asked now. He stared at the road unfurling ahead of them as the truck's headlights cast a path and didn't speak again until they arrived at his trailer.

"I want to buy a couple of Oxy if you got any," John said when they had pulled to the top of the driveway.

"Now bullshit, I ain't fronting you nothing. You got money?"

"I got a trade, let me run up here and grab it."

Sweetie's truck exhaled as he pulled the key from the ignition. John jogged up the steps to his front door. Moonlight and a chill spun through the air on top of the mountain ridge. The Chevy's engine creaked and sizzled as it cooled down. Sweetie strained his ears to listen as a hound stopped barking and settled back in as the night grew colder. At the bottom of the hill where the road began, a single light glowed dirty yellow atop a wooden pole with streaks of rot and splinters all the way up.

The front door of the trailer opened and closed again with a soft thud. John sidestepped back down the steps to the truck, a small satchel over his shoulders. He climbed into the truck next to Sweetie and pulled the door together without slamming it.

John hadn't worked in weeks, especially since he'd been running around with Case. The only reason he could figure Sweetie came and got him was because the old man needed some money. John was of the mind that pill dealers were all the same, only caring about money owed or what a body has to trade. Sweetie didn't care that he had fallen so far in this life.

John opened the flap of his bag and passed a shining .38 Special revolver across the cab of the truck.

"What you want for it?" Sweetie asked.

"Two."

"State boys looking for this?"

"That's a high-dollar pistol, Sweetie. Just give me a hundred even. You know you can get a lot more than that out of it."

"You could at least act like it ain't hot."

"That's Daddy's old Smith & Wesson. He's rolling in his grave right now. Why you always interrogating me? Like you think I ain't good for nothing. I thought you wasn't stuck up like that." John locked his eyes forward out the front window of the truck, refusing to give the man in the driver's seat any more authority over him than he already possessed.

Sweetie was focused on the wheel gun. He wiped the mirrored finish of the pistol and thumbed the release until its cylinder flipped out and then he eyeballed the empty barrel. He snapped it shut and stuffed it deep beneath the truck seat. Sweetie fingered in his shirt pocket and pinched out a wad of cash. He peeled off enough twenties to pay John for the revolver. Before he handed the cash over, John folded his arms across his chest and twisted his cracking lips together.

"Just keep it and give me a few of them Oxy like I asked for. I owe you more than that anyways." The words snapped from his thin mouth.

Most of the night had set in, but somewhere below that single light post and its fading glow an owl cooed in the dark. Sweetie's mind settled on the bird's call. He remembered hunting deer with his father and uncles when he was younger. They once came on an old hoot owl hid out in a barn loft. Sweetie's skin pricked up when he looked upon the great bird. Eerily long in its gliding movements, like some creature not of this time or space. It stared down into Sweetie the way another man would, the way something more than a man might, beyond the murky surface of his green eyes that swelled wide as the river. Sweetie had squared down on the owl and put a slug through its chest sending bloody feathers floating down among the men. He still didn't know quite for sure why he killed that owl.

Sweetie pocketed his cash and dug into his boot for John's pills. The younger man palmed them tightly and scrambled back up the porch steps with the dark of night on his back.

CHAPTER FORTY-SIX

John hadn't planned on accepting that invitation to church, but after rehab hadn't worked he didn't know what else to do. He was tired and couldn't bring himself to throw away that pamphlet he'd be given. The fall had faded away from memory and a cold December had settled in when he visited one Sunday. Something about those people made him feel cleaner than he'd felt in a long time. He had only gone a few times before he broke down at the preacher's heels. Anne had wanted to quit these pills and she never got the chance. He didn't want to face the same cold fate.

The only person John decided to invite to his baptism was Sweetie. He stood on Sweetie's porch and stared him in the eyes stone-cold sober. Sweetie spat into the yard and chuckled.

"Well, hell. Guess I'll be missing you for a little while. Is there enough Spirit out there to cure a dope-sick man? You'll need a lot of grace," Sweetie scratched at his armpit and crossed his ankles in front of where he sat, "from what I know about you anyways."

The smell of burning wood wafted over John, it carried from the furnace in Sweetie's front room. He listened to dead weeds and cold branches rustling against the wind as he realized he didn't have anything else to say to Sweetie Goodins.

Since he'd been sober, John had got a job at a factory. He snapped small metal parts onto a wide steel rack that was lifted by a big muscle man who hung it on a rail and ran it through a coating machine. The factory floor stayed hot even during the winter. John worked third shift with the moon in the sky. Outside the steel doors it was snowing and the wind howled. But inside the furnaces swelled with flames and the smell of chemicals danced on the air.

His gloves had torn at the fingertips after his first week. He wiped at his brow and sweat stung the corner of his eyes. He could feel his bowels beginning to work loose. John was always amazed at how stopped up pills kept a person's guts. His mouth always felt dry now and his hands seemed to always shake a little.

The short little plump woman working behind John was revved up to top end. From the first day she talked to him he had taken her for some kind of a speeder. She was talking a hundred miles an hour and snapping those parts on like he couldn't believe. Never missing a beat. There was another man, he was probably in his sixties or so. He kept his fingernails grown real long and his palm had lingered in John's when they first shook hands. John thought this job would keep him away from other addicts and people like Tim Stevens, but he wasn't sure it was too much different than working the sawmill.

When the following Sunday came, he glanced in his rearview mirror one last time. He rubbed his face with his palms and wiped his nose with his hand to knock out any hangers. Giving the lap of his pants one last brush, he stepped out of the little banged-up Honda he had bought with his first paycheck. It was cold and rainy as he walked towards the church-house steps. The narrow rectangular parking lot was packed full that day. He reckoned the preacher must've sent out a whole string of emails to rope this many people into coming to a doper's confession. John knew there were to be faces in the crowd that he had robbed and lied to. Some maybe worse than that.

The wind was sharp against his cheeks as he stood before the large, wooden doors. An old farm truck piddled up the road past the church and then it was only John and the choice to open the door. He could have just as easily turned back to the Honda, rolled it up to the salvage yard, and taken the junk money over to Sweetie or Tim or maybe Case knew someone new with some stout dope. His hand clasped the cold brass handle and he pulled it open against the drab gust of winter.

Once the service had started, John marched stiff legged to the front of the sanctuary. His khakis were dirty with deep wrinkles. He wore a blue-and-white-striped shirt with the cuffs buttoned tight around his wrists. The preacher stood a head taller than John. His shoulders were square and rigid in a charcoal-gray suit jacket. He clapped one of his giant paws square between John's shoulder blades. The step up onto the pulpit couldn't have been more than a few inches high, but John took it in a great long stride as though he had just stepped up an entire cliff face with nowhere to get a toehold. His head had been buzzed clean for the occasion. He could feel his armpits sweating as he took in the church crowd.

"Our guest John and I have an announcement we'd like to make. We've all known this young man in our community for quite some time now."

The preacher paused and wiped at the corner of an eye. He gazed over the congregation and a smile broke across his solemn stare.

"No, it has not always been a righteous path that he has followed, but brothers and sisters we are here today to tell you that he has found the Truth!" The preacher's voice raised with excitement.

John kicked off his boots, picked one leg up, and swung it over into a cattle trough turned baptismal. The water was warmed by a metal rod that dipped in over the side. His dirty khakis drank up water and turned dark brown. He stared out at mostly faces from his elder generation, some kids who were too young to be paying any attention, and a few younger married couples.

"I am sorry for what I have done. To all of you. Y'all know enough of my past that there ain't much need for me to tell you. I've been chained down to them pills. Prowling around like a rabid animal. If you ever dared to have me around, you know I was just as likely to rob you blind as to smile at you." John's mouth felt tight around so many words.

The skin on his hands seemed splotchy and damp beneath the white light. Sweetie Goodins was nowhere to be seen despite his invitation. Lucy and his mother sat front row. Mamaw Perley wore a flowing, floral print dress with green leaves so bright and sharp they drowned out all the other colors. Lucy looked puny; a hymnal rested in her lap. John wondered if the harsh edges of the leather-bound book were heavy on her precious knees. When she noticed her father looking at her, she dropped her head and stared into the carpet beneath her feet.

John stretched his arms out and clasped his fingers at the top of his head before lowering his hands into clenched fists at his sides. The preacher held a single open palm toward the flat white lights that shone down from the ceiling of the sanctuary.

"John Perley, do you repent of your sins and acknowledge your need of a Savior?"

"Yes, I do," John said.

"And have you put your faith in Jesus Christ as your Lord?"

"With all of my heart."

"Today we bury the old John Perley with Christ and raise you up unto a new life! I baptize you in the name of the Father, the Son, and the Holy Spirit!"

The preacher grasped John's left hand and covered John's nose with his other while he dunked him beneath the warm, clear water of the cattle trough. John came out sopping wet. His button-down shirt looked two or three sizes too big on his scrawny frame. Mamaw Perley sobbed and the other old women praised God. The piano rang to life and the church thrummed into song. John stepped out to the carpeted floor of the stage and scuffled to a door at the side of the sanctuary, dribbling water across the crimson rug under his bare toes. He could hear as the singing tapered off towards the last verse, and the preacher cleared his throat to begin the sermon.

With a change of clothes, John watched himself in the bathroom mirror. He gripped his fresh-shaven neck and rubbed his palm against his cheek. He still didn't trust himself. He tried to feel something. He wondered if Sweetie was home.

The sermon had already started when John eased back out to the door he'd exited through. He peered through the cracked door from the edge of the sanctuary. His eyes searched for an empty seat, but the only open place was right up front. He knew all the church members would be gathering up after the service to shake his hand, embrace him, and welcome him. They would slap his back and make jokes about the past as though it were really erased. John was finding it hard to believe his transgressions would be so easily forgotten. Some of the older women would hug him and cry and he'd go along with it for their sake more than his own.

He quietly stepped to the front row. John's fresh jeans were dry and crisp against his thighs. He rubbed his palms flat against his pant legs. The cattle trough sat emptier now at the preacher's side. The water still sloshed back and forth slightly. The preacher cried out a name John didn't recognize. "Lazarus, come forth!"

John could feel his stomach turning inside his flesh. The rows of light above the congregation bared down on him. Sweat beaded in swollen drops on his forehead. He thought for sure he was going to vomit. He concentrated on not chucking bile all over the plush red carpet. Just when he thought he'd suppressed it, his gut bottomed out. He clinched tight and held his hands to his stomach. He knew now that there wasn't an option, he had to go. The preacher smiled out at the church. John's face was set like stone. He stood and slipped through the same side door, through the narrow hallway, into the bathroom where he had just changed. His khakis and the striped button-down were still hanging from the doorknob in a gray plastic grocery bag, tied off at the top, dripping water onto the bathroom tiles, forming a pool. John yanked his jeans down to his ankles and finally let go.

Before he left the bathroom, John glanced in the mirror one last time. He wiped at his nose and dried his hands on the back of his pant legs. John stared down the hall back towards the sanctuary, he could hear the piano starting up for the invitation hymn. They'd be ready to throw their arms around him in praise. He didn't have it in him to step back out there.

John took the side door out. He hurried across the parking lot hoping not to hear anyone calling him back to the church. The wind was sharper than it had been earlier, but the blanketed clouds above were starting to break apart. The sun was trickling through, its rays blinding those who looked upon them as they mixed into the silver linings of the clouds.

CHAPTER FORTY-SEVEN

Lucy watched the telephone poles flicker past as her father drove wild-eyed, his shoulders tightening as they cut into a deep corner of the road. Lucy swayed in the seat next to him. John fiddled with the heater switch, back and forth and back again. After his baptism, her mamaw had been leaving her at home more often, which she didn't really mind too much.

"Piece of shit," John said. He turned both knobs to full blast and let it be.

Lucy liked their old car better. She liked the chrome switch and the way it jutted out of the heavy brown wood panel at an angle. She missed the crack in the dashboard staring her in the face while she picked at the broken plastic with her fingernail.

The little Honda bounced over the curb into Case's driveway and followed soft ruts in the dirt and grass until they parked at Case's back door. Lucy could see cardboard and aluminum foil sealing the insides of the house's windows. Case cracked the door and stepped out to sit on the doorstep, folding his arms around him and tucking his knees up in front of his chest. Lucy noticed the man's eye was swollen and bruised.

"Who whooped you around like that?" her father asked.

"Fucker up at the sawmill thought I stole something out of his truck," Case said.

"You been working for Tim?"

"Only when I got to."

"Y'all been getting into anything?"

"Just trying to make it. Tim's about the only person we know to go to anymore."

"Come up to the mountain sometime, I'll get Sweetie to stop by with some."

Lucy half listened to the men, but mostly watched chickens pecking around in the yard next door. The birds strutted up and down a row of chain-link fence. They gently cawed and scratched. A cold morning drizzle started to fall around them. Lucy rolled her window down and stuck her arm out into the crisp droplets of what felt like mercy, her hairs pricked upright down the length of her arm in the brittle rain.

Above the chickens pecking, the clouds sailed like lost men and women searching for safe shores, huddled together in clusters, stretching themselves between one horizon and another. Lucy felt her own horizon had been broken, but she couldn't say exactly where or when, like a melted sunrise leaking into the shadows of the mountains. Shadows with a hunger that wouldn't wain. Not in these years of her life, not on this day.

As the winter ached by, Lucy didn't forget about her mother though she tried. It would have been like trying to forget about a severed finger, there was still a nub hanging and old habits die hard. She would awake on certain mornings and step down the hallway with a lightness in her stride, with a call to her mother cradled in the back of her throat before the sudden realization gripped her young frame of mind. Tonight, she clutched the last birthday card she'd ever received in her mother's handwriting to her chest:

Dear Lucy girl,

Happy birthday! We are proud of the little lady you are becoming. We love you so much.

Mommy and Daddy

The kerosene heater pitched waves of heat up toward the ceiling of the trailer. A blanket hung in the doorframe to the hallway trapping the heat in the living room where she and her father slept together. Her father lay alone on the couch, numb beneath a heavy quilt, his muddy boots propped up on one armrest of the couch with his neck bent unnaturally against the other. Lucy's mattress had been pulled out of her bedroom and now sat snug in the corner of the living room. A pulsing orange glow climbed the white walls around Lucy. She wiggled her toes beneath her blanket and squeezed her eyes shut, her cheeks warm. She was drifting to sleep when the kerosene heater popped loudly as the fuel gauge struck empty, shadows and flames no longer dancing along the drywall. The heater's round metal belly groaned in the cool black room and Lucy shivered all alone.

CHAPTER FORTY-EIGHT

The factory cut John loose after a few weeks. He hadn't been surprised. Odd jobs with Sweetie paid well, but the sawmill was the only consistent work around. Kentucky's winter days were milder than most places, and that meant there was still logging being done. All he had to do was show up and he'd be put to work.

Tim acted like he didn't know him after John had ripped the man off for the fentanyl. They never spoke a word to one another and that suited John Perley just fine.

Dried gray poplar planks splintered into John's forearms as he carried them away from the mill to a neat pile. He dropped the wood stack at his feet and turned to grab another armload. He watched Case from the corner of his eye. Case's pupils bobbled in his head without seeing what was right in front of them. Even John knew Case had taken a turn for the worse. The sky was cold and flat and blue above. Treetops looked stenciled across the horizon. John pulled his jeans up and cinched his belt a notch tighter around his waist.

That weekend Sweetie and the two Estes brothers sat around John Perley's kitchen table. It felt like old times in some way. Lucy was playing in her room at the back of the trailer. Case sat with his legs sprawled out wide. He wore a baggy pair of overalls with a hoodie underneath. His long hair hung past his shoulders, dry and frizzy. James kept popping his head up, only to lull back over until his forehead kissed the painted-white tabletop again. John stood leaning against the kitchen sink smoking a cigarette. Sweetie tapped his finger against his knee and talked to John like the other two weren't present.

"I can't hardly trust Tim a lick anymore, he's fooling with that fentanyl shit too much. It ain't no good," Sweetie said.

"You're just pissed he's been taking your business." John played with his lighter. He'd cuff one hand and let butane flow into his hollow fist, then he'd strike the wheel and a ball of fire would fill his palm in a quick flash.

"I gotta take a piss." Case said.

Lucy's arms and legs tensed as she sensed someone walking towards the back of the trailer down the narrow hall that led to her bedroom. She fixed her mouth in a tight line and turned from her dolls to face the bedroom door.

Case Estes stood in the frame of the cheap vinyl trim. His overalls sagged on his tall bony frame. His dirty long hair lay plaited in two strands over each shoulder. His beard was auburn and curled up in tight wads all the way down his neck to his Adam's apple.

Lucy couldn't breathe. She flattened her palms against the carpet and shifted her weight to her heels. He stayed rooted at the threshold of the bedroom. Lucy could hear her father and Sweetie talking back and forth at each other in the kitchen. Case smiled at Lucy, waved with one hand, and then put both hands in his overall pockets. His lips were flaky and dry from the cold weather. A split in his top lip had cracked open and began to bleed a little bit when he grinned a broad mouthful of yellowed teeth, mostly straight, but some stained with dark marks. Lucy's bluff melted away when her mouth wrinkled into a frown. She wanted to scream, but it was as though a pair of her father's vice grips had clamped around her slender throat.

The tall man's beady eyes flicked around the room and back to Lucy. Her heart pounded in her sternum as he came into the room and crouched down in front of her. She turned to her bedroom window. She wanted nothing more than one of her moths to be dancing across its clear surface, but there was only the black of night. She could feel the man behind her. He hugged her close until her back pressed against his chest. She could feel the buttons of his overalls poking into her shoulder blade. He reached a hand around and pinched the child's nipple through her thin T-shirt. He twisted the soft of her flesh until tears filled her eyes and she was afraid that piece of her would rot and fall off. She still couldn't cry out for her father, for Mr. Goodins, for anyone. She heard footsteps, someone else coming through the kitchen. She prayed it was her father. Case's shape sank into the darkness of her window's reflection. She heard the bathroom door click shut and turned to stare at the door to the hallway. Just as suddenly her father appeared in the doorway.

"You alright back here, Lucy girl?" John asked.

"I'm just playing," she said.

Lucy's hands were still and relaxed, but her legs felt like they were rattling around in their sockets. She thought she could feel a little bit of blood pooling underneath her shirt. She worried for a second that her father would notice and then she thought to tell him about the tall man coming in but without understanding why she stopped, afraid to speak of the moment.

CHAPTER FORTY-NINE

When Lucy opened her eyes the next morning her shirt was stuck to her chest where the blood had dried. The room was mostly dark, but her window glowed in the low morning blue. Lucy tried to go back to sleep and forget, to slip back into her dreams where cowboys talked tough to one another, but her only worry was lush rows of melons and cucumbers planted on a gentle hillside. This morning was not the same as the morning her daddy cut his finger off. It was not even the same as when she found out her mommy had died for good. Lucy's eyes watched the ceiling above her bed. Little sunbursts of white paint hung frozen forever just before they had the chance to drip down to the carpet below. It was not fully dawn outside yet, but the girl could tell from the soft light at her window that soon the sun would creep up over the hill behind her house. The cold December morning would be foggy for some time then the day would turn stale. The grating wind would pass over them the same as it did the rocks and the stream. Maybe come spring she could dip her feet in the creek again, but she had no desire to wait. She wanted to go now. Now, before her father woke up and the blank sun cast its careless white glare on the landscape. Now, while there was still blood staining her shirt and she could still feel the long-haired man's hands burning her skin. If she could just find the strength to move, to rise and step out into the bitter winter air that sifted through the trailer walls.

She climbed out of bed to peek into the yard, hoping a moth or two may still be perched against the windowsill.

Lucy lost her breath when she broke the seal of the curtain. She was afraid at first, the massive creature's breath fogged the frosted window. Lucy loomed, enamored by the beauty of its magnificence. It's sheer brutishness, standing assured and strong. Graceful in the morning haze. Close enough for Lucy to see the gloss over its eye, to see the wetness clinging to its snout. She could have counted each point of its rack that sat atop its head.

It was an elk. She had seen plenty of Turkeyfoot deer—her father never failed to point them out when he saw one. Even if they were driving, he'd slow the car to a crawl and gesture until she spotted them. This was no deer. Sensing her at the window the elk trotted a safe distance away and perked its ears to listen for any threat. She held her breath and waited until the animal let its guard down again. It grazed in the willowed plants along the edge of the yard. She wanted to reach for it, but knew there was no way she could touch it as the glass was between them. Behind the animal, oak-tree roots shot out of a slipping bank's soft dirt where the rain had cut miniature valleys of mud. A gnarled root hung yellow and red from where her father had struck it time and time again with the blade of an axe out of anger. The creature bellowed and it was a sound like Lucy had never heard.

The edges of the morning view outside her window were soft and fuzzy until it all snapped into focus. Crystalizing in Lucy's eyes. Like glass shattering in the pit of her mind. Then without a sound or another glance in her direction, the elk stepped up the bank and vanished into the tree line. Her heart pounded in her chest, and she took a deep breath.

Lucy was afraid the men might have spent the night. She peeked into the living room and spotted only her father snoring on the couch with his quilt pulled up over his head and his boots sticking out. She snatched her jacket and pulled on a pair of old tennis shoes before running out the front door and gently shutting it behind her. She scrambled across her yard and slid down the bank to the creek, hanging onto sprouting saplings, young in the earth, bending in her grasp as she found footing on her way down and then snapping back upright when she turned loose to skid down into the pebbles and mud.

The water trickled across mossy stones. The ground was gritty beneath the soles of her shoes. She slid her sneakers off at the edge of the stream and buried her heels into the mud and sand. She dug her toes in and flexed them. The stream was cold rushing over her ankles. The girl wondered how long she had until the sun came up. How long until she had to go back and face her life again. Lucy stared to the treetops. She wondered where the moths flew in the morning to rest. Whether they perched in the highest limbs or floated from porch light to porch light, searching for a door to cling to. She wondered where the elk was now and how many more of them stalked the mountain silently like one of the mythological creatures her teacher spoke about. Lucy felt like she could move whole mountains if she wanted to. If only she lived like the moths and was not afraid to fly down to the light. The morning she found out her mother had died she felt guilty for the relief that washed over her, as though one of the raging storms she was caught between had finally fallen silent and she could fully surrender to the tide of the other. The choice made for her, one less chest to watch for shallow breaths. Lucy had kept her eyes peeled all week for a moth that might remind her of her mother, but none came. She took the elk as a sign more lovely than she could have ever imagined.

When she walked back up to the house her father was sitting at the top of the porch steps smoking a cigarette. She knew the smoke wasn't good for her, but she loved the smell of it. It was reliable at least. The rich, warm scent let her know that at least her daddy was still here for her despite his flaws.

"Where you been at, Lucy? I was starting to get worried. I thought maybe your Mamaw came and got you."

"I just wanted to go to the creek for a while before the sun came up."

"Ain't it too cold for that?"

"No, it feels good when it's cool," Lucy said. She sat down at the foot of the steps below her daddy. "That man with the nasty hair came into my room last night. He pinched me really hard."

"He what?"

"It happened fast. He came in when I was playing and pinched me on my chest. I bled a little bit." Lucy wanted to keep it to herself, but she knew she had to say something no matter how afraid she was.

"Show me." John's cigarette was burning down to the place where he held it between two knuckles. The ash curled up before it flaked off and floated down to the wooden step. Lucy pulled her shirt up and showed him the bruised and bloodied circle of flesh. Lucy waited for him to say something, but he only flicked his cigarette into the yard.

CHAPTER FIFTY

As winter waned the grass began to grow again and Sweetie couldn't have been happier to have something to keep him busy. His father had been in the nursing home for a long while now, and he hadn't spoken to John after he heard what happened to Lucy. Sweat stung his eyes and he could feel his neck reddening under the spring sun. Wet clumps of grass clung to the legs of his pants. Sweetie wiped his cheek with a forearm. He was stooped down on the slant between the gravel and the fence line to catch his breath, one knee bent under him and the other keeping a foothold to step back up onto the road. He tried to stand, but the slope of the hill was slicker than he thought from rain. He took one step up the slope towards his truck before slipping down and smearing mud all over the lap of his pants. He cursed and threw the Weed eater up to the road.

The spring weather had left Turkeyfoot a mess. Some late winter storms had frozen the mountain and now warmer weather and heavy rain were thawing everything back out. The toe of Sweetie's boot dug into the sopping muddy grass, and he used both hands to pull himself up the rest of the way. He snatched the Weed eater up, heaved it into the bed of his truck, and slammed the tailgate shut. The setting sun looked molten against the purpling skyline; a dark red orb filled to the brim. Sweetie hooked the chain around the old farm gate but didn't fasten the lock. The old man might have been gone, but he could still feel his father cursing him about locking up properly. He jingled the loose change in his pocket, the bright red sun ball had burned down to a dull orange. He thought of Lucy Perley and her father. Two lights of their own, one just beginning to glow and one about to burn out for good if he didn't change. Sweetie counted off enough quarters for a pop at the corner stop as he walked back to his truck.

Even if he wasn't completely sober, John had the place looking a lot better. The trailer looked cleaner than Sweetie had ever seen it and the porch was a mixture of fresh new planks with aged ones that were still sturdy enough to stand. He walked up to knock, but before he got to the door Lucy opened it to meet him.

"What are you doing here?" Lucy said. She hadn't seen Sweetie or Case or any of them around since she told her daddy what the longhaired man had done to her.

"Well, that ain't no way to say hello, is it?" Sweetie was stunned by the authority behind the child's voice. He knew she had been forced to grow up fast in this life of hers, but she was still so small even for a nine-year-old.

"Daddy is in the backyard working," she said. He could see the girl's mother in her small dark eyes.

"I brought this for you." Sweetie sat a sweaty can of cream soda on the porch rail.

"Mr. Goodins, why do people like to take drugs so much?" Her sharp brown eyes searched the man's face.

"Honey, a lot of them are good people, they just got a bad habit." Sweetie turned back down the steps.

In the back he found John, bony chested and hollow inside. A lone figure sweating over the sawhorse again, marking and cutting only to mark and cut again. John's head snapped up at Sweetie as soon as he rounded the corner of the trailer.

"What the hell you want?" John spat across the wood planks into the grass at Sweetie's boots.

"Just checking in on y'all I guess."

"We're fine, we don't need nobody worrying about us."

"You heard from Case any?" Sweetie asked.

"No." John powered up the saw and ran it through another slab of poplar.

"That little girl needs you, John. You're all she's got in this world. Don't do nothing stupid."

"I'm getting sick and tired of everyone telling me how to take care of my own damned daughter."

"I ain't trying to tell you nothing, I'm just as pissed as you over what happened. Sickos like him always get what's coming to them. Just let it set awhile."

"I reckon it's been setting, ain't it? What am I supposed to do about it? It's my own damned fault."

Sweetie knew John wanted him to leave. He didn't want the man's wrath turning on him, so he headed back to his truck and drove home to sit and stew on his own accord.

CHAPTER FIFTY-ONE

John's veins branched down his forearm like a good fork in the river with plenty of creeks branching off. He poked at a plump one in the crook of his elbow, pale green beneath his soft skin.

He already had a few scars from healing track marks and recently he'd been picking at a fresh scab. It would usually stop bleeding if he held a tissue over it for a minute. In a little while when he was coming back down, he would pick at it more and it'd start back to bleeding again, a thin trail of red, the only thing reminding him that life still flowed inside his body.

Sweetie wouldn't fool with Case and his brother hardly to begin with. But ever since he'd heard about Case going into that little girl's room, he told John very plainly to never bring them around him again or he'd be cut off the same as they were. Case and James had gone crazier than hell. John didn't even hardly like running with them anymore, but addiction made for some odd company. The last he heard they'd been copping crystal from the jugheads down on the riverbank. Big country boys, cooking cloudy shards of meth out of the mouth of a holler before you started up the mountain road. They took turns blocking the gate to the only road in and out with big jacked-up trucks on fat off-road tires. They'd all load up together in another one's truck and ride down to the bare shack where they kept their little operation under strict lock and key. John wasn't that desperate yet, but he figured it'd only be a matter of time before he got sick again. And when he was sick he was willing to try just about anything to stop it.

CHAPTER FIFTY-TWO

"I told you I didn't want nothing to do with these sick fucks!"

As soon as Sweetie walked into John's living room and seen the Estes brothers sitting on the couch he had started cursing John to pieces.

"Listen to me, Sweetie, just listen to me." John held his arms around himself and paced the floor.

"You ain't listening to me! I told you I ain't got any more pills for none of y'all. Give me what you owe me so I can get out of here," Sweetie said.

"You ain't listening to me, Sweetie. I only need one and I'll call you later this evening to pay you everything I owe." John tapped his heel and shook his head at the old man.

Sweetie felt sick to his stomach. He thought the young man was about to cry.

"I got a big payday for us tonight, guaranteed. We're good for it, man," Case chimed in. He had just finished splitting a thirty with his brother. James didn't seem to care about the conversation happening in front of him, just tilted his head back and closed his eyes. Case stood up and stepped towards the center of the room where Sweetie and John stood.

The pocketknife in Sweetie's hip pocket was the one he used to clean his nails and cut down the callouses he kept getting on his heel. The blade was only about three inches long, but it was straight and sharp, with a point like a toothpick. Sweetie unfolded it and held his index finger against the spine of the blade as he thrust it out at Case's scruffy neck. He held the boy by a matted lock of hair with his other hand and firmly pressed the edge against Case's flesh. A thin line of blood trickled down over Case's patchy beard. Sweetie pulled back and spat in the man's face.

"You ever look at that little girl again and I'll spill every damned drop of you out in the dirt." Sweetie clenched his teeth around each word as it left his lips.

James had nodded off on the couch with his hands folded between his legs. John didn't dare speak, he stared down at the floor still tapping his foot. Case stood still. His eyes gazed down upon the old man he could've easily overpowered. He finally wiped Sweetie's spit off his cheek and smeared it onto the front of his hoodie.

Even though Sweetie didn't give him anything, John called early evening like he said he would. He asked Sweetie to pick him up down by the railroad tracks. Sweetie found him walking down a gravel road up under the bypass. He pulled up his truck next to the younger man and then rolled down his window. On one side of them the river glistened, on the other, somewhere through the woods, a train clunked empty carts behind it, blaring its whistle into the shining spring day. Bright orange ticks of spray paint climbed one of the concrete pillars that held the bridge above them, each one marking how high the river had swelled in years past.

John had called just asking Sweetie to give him a ride back from town. No sooner than Sweetie had rolled down the window he started asking again for some thirties.

"You know I'm good for it, Sweetie! I always get you back one way or another." John sounded strung out. His eyes were bloodshot and his skin pale. "Don't be this way, man."

He had come up with a big plan to sell them for Sweetie as repayment of what he owed. When Sweetie laughed in his face, John screamed and stomped and kicked the Chevrolet's fender.

"Walk your ass back home if you're gonna act like a fool." Sweetie rolled the window back up and started to shift the truck into drive.

John slapped his palms against the tinted window. Sweetie stared into John's mouth on the other side of the glass as it shaped out muffled curses against the closed door. John balled up a fist and bounced it off the window—the skin off his middle knuckle peeled back and bled, but he hammered the glass again. Blue shards scratched Sweetie's cheek and tiny slivers of glass landed in his combed hair still stiff with pomade. Light came through the fist-shaped hole. The rest of the window was still held together by the thin sheet of black tint. John's fist dripped blood into Sweetie's lap before he ripped his arm back through. The color red ribboned down the webbed glass and into the truck's door panel.

A gust of wind crashed through like a wave shoving against sandy shores somewhere far away from Turkeyfoot. Fresh blooming leaves rippled across the treetops. Up above, semis roared across the bypass. Barely blooming tree limbs stood against the skyline like the dead reaching back for life. Sweetie swore he caught a smell of rotting mulberries hanging in the air.

CHAPTER FIFTY-THREE

Once Sweetie got back home, he swept out most of the broken glass and wiped the blood off his door panel. Inside he flopped out on the couch and pulled his hat down snug over his eyes. Dust hung on the air. The man stared down at the floor and held his hands together at his stomach. He rubbed his thumb over his knuckles where the ring from his father's dresser used to sit. Sweetie laid down and propped his feet up on the armrest and pulled his cap down tighter to block out any light.

He dreamed again of his father and when they would hunt rabbits in the wintertime. The dogs whined, moaned, and begged to be let loose. Sweetie's father unlatched the janky door and the two beagles squeezed out of the crate at once. They hopped down from the bed of the truck into a puddle of mud. Their ears flopped and one of them shook a chill out of its spine. After that they never looked back. They sprinted from fencerow to brush pile to thickets like bees working a hive, their noses rarely leaving the frozen ground. Him and his father finished off a thermos of coffee. Steam billowed out from the rims of their cups before breaking apart in the wind. They loaded their guns and followed down the field behind the hounds.

Sweetie stomped piles of branches and kicked at patches of weeds. They marched the length of the farm like soldiers, dodging cow patties as though they were land mines and keeping their heads on a tight swivel.

The old beagle got a hit and started howling, the younger dog fell in with her yipping. Sweetie could no longer feel the wind smacking his face numb, his back stiffened as his mind slipped to thoughts of the warm bed at home.

The dogs tracked the scent through a barbed-wire fence. They disappeared into a tangle of briar with their blood-tipped tails pointing to the sky. His father propped his gun against the fence post, a barb snagging his jacket as he climbed over. He took off through the weeds to where the dogs moaned. Sweetie didn't cross behind him, but instead followed the fencerow with hopes of cutting them off on their way back around.

As Sweetie walked, he thumbed the safety of the 20 gauge. His father was out of sight somewhere beyond the trees. The gun was heavy in his grip and the howls were distant now. He ran a hand along the twining wire; it sagged loosely in places. His fingers wandered along rusty patches.

Sweetie pinched a barb.

He pinched it hard between his thumb and fingertip. Hard enough to feel it stab into his skin, but never enough to bring blood.

Suddenly, he could hear the dogs rounding back on the other side. He wrapped his fist tightly around the strand of wire and let the sharp points tear into his palm. The hair on Sweetie's arms and neck pricked up. The freezing wind burned his bare knuckles raw.

Three shotgun blasts split the air as fast as his father could work the pump action.

"Coming your way!" he called out somewhere through the trees.

Sweetie pulled his hand back and the metal scratched a thin line into his flesh. The cold gun made him wish for a pair of gloves. On the other side of the fence, he could see the rabbit. Her coat was dirty brown with tufts of crisp white on her chest. The dogs were still running through the brush, trailing the scent. He brought the barrel up, placed the bead, and his shoulder bucked behind the crack of the gun.

He missed.

The hot smell of gunpowder flooded Sweetie's nose as the spent shell hit the ground and another slid into the chamber. The second shot cut the rabbit down. The dogs fell silent. The world around him was muffled except for the animal's desperate squeal. He took a breath and climbed through the fence. The rabbit's fur was soaked in blood. Her sides fluttered for air. She looked Sweetie in the eyes as he reached down and plucked her up by the back limbs.

His father appeared from the tree line now. He seemed to have aged ten years since last season. His face was knotted in the wind. His wrinkles and scars cut deep and dry. The dogs pleaded for a taste of the rabbit. Their tails swept from side to side. One of the beagles stood on her hind legs and snapped her jaws.

"You sure I didn't get that one? I swear I saw its tail end kick sideways." His father laughed and struggled to catch his breath as he pulled a pack of cigarettes from his coat pocket. He cuffed his hands and fought with the wind before the lighter caught. He took a hard drag and the rich smell drifted to Sweetie's nose despite the sharp breeze.

"Didn't look like you hurt him too bad to me." Sweetie meant to laugh, but his words came out flat.

They both stared at the animal hanging in his grip. Its whining was stuttered and shallow now, frantically begging for either life or death, Sweetie was unsure of which. With its joints gritty in his fist, smashed from the shot, he brought the barrel of the gun down across the rabbit's skull. Once, twice, until the screaming stopped.

CHAPTER FIFTY-FOUR

Sweetie hadn't run any pills since the winter. He mostly spent his days walking around the old farm and getting sentimental about the way it used to be. Some days he visited his father, but he was just as likely to lie up on the couch all day.

He sat at his kitchen table drinking a cup of coffee and stewing over what had happened to Lucy. There were days he thought about killing Case Estes. His phone vibrated against his thigh. He reached into his pocket and saw that John was calling him. He hadn't heard from him since they'd seen each other at the rail yard. If the boy was using, he wasn't getting it from Sweetie. But Sweetie didn't know why he would be calling him now.

He silenced the phone and tossed it to the center of the table. Sweetie pulled on his boots and walked outside to a cool spring morning.

Outside he kicked one of his truck's back tires and stood at the edge of the gravel with his hands stuffed in his pockets. The sky was clear and blue today. Sweetie stared at the line of fence posts coming up the edge of the driveway. The barbed wire was rusted nearly in two in some places. The posts were dead and some had fallen over completely, crumbling beneath the weight of their rot.

A muddy slope steepened downwards into a pit where cows used to drink rainwater years ago. Sweetie pressed the palms of his hands into his eye sockets and held them there until his vision became starry. He took off walking down the slope to the old pasture, the same path his father walked many mornings on his way to feed and water his herd. Sweetie's dreams came back to him, and he wondered if he might jump a rabbit simply walking through the brush. This was not the place of his dreams, but it could just as easily have been. This small piece of land had ingrained itself into the man's being. He didn't know where he would be without such an anchor. Lost and frightened, more so than he felt even with this foundation to stand on.

Sweetie stopped where the grass gave way to a soft bank of clay and crouched down. He picked a blade of grass and turned it over between his fingers. The evening grew darker every minute. Sweetie's father had been twenty when he was born, and they had grown old with each other.

"No count for nothing," Sweetie said to himself.

He sat in the emptiness around his words. Spoken to nobody. They had never said much to begin with, but now he missed his father's rare remarks of wisdom. This farm had once been a beautiful place to live. There was hardly more a body could ask for. But now it had been worn down and neglected. Sweetie had never cared for it as his parents had. They knew beyond his years what this place meant.

He wondered when his own end may come. Whether or not it was at the bottom of this solemn hill after living a life on high across the ridge. Maybe he would walk back home, and the hour would pass over him in the silence of the night. Sweetie missed his father more than he imagined he would.

When he walked back to the house he decided to go through more of his father's belongings. From the closet he dug out an old shoebox full of scraps of notebook paper with Bible verses haphazardly written anywhere there was blank space. Whoever had ransacked the house hadn't seen much value in them. They were scraps from Isaiah, Jeremiah, and Ezekiel. Prophets and vessels of God's message. Some pages were crumpled while others were folded into neat triangles, like a paper football from grade school.

Sweetie wanted to kill Case Estes for what he had done to that little girl. He knew it wasn't his place to do so, but that didn't stop him from the notion.

CHAPTER FIFTY-FIVE

Tim and Sweetie hadn't seen each other in months. Sweetie was surprised when Tim invited him to come inside the kitchen and sit down for a spell. It was just evening. Sweetie had called Tim that morning to see if they could talk.

"Where's your old lady?" Sweetie asked.

"She's taking a little vacation. She was becoming a bit too dependent on her morning medicine," Tim said. "But how are you, Mr. Goodins?"

"I've honestly never been better."

"Why do you figure?"

"It's like a burden has been lifted off me. I finally know why He said the Son of Man has no place to lay his head."

"You've been reading from scripture?"

"Only thing left to do sitting at the house all alone. Picked up Dad's old family Bible for once."

"So, what do you think?"

"I've been trying to hold on to a world that won't last. A world done gone to the wayside."

"It's not much, is it?"

"No. It's not."

"Like you said, it's all passing on anyways," Tim said. He took a long drink of his coffee and sat the cup on the counter between them.

"I need a bag of that fentanyl. You still got some?"

"I thought you didn't want to fool with it any?"

"I had a change of heart."

"That's two changes."

"I just ain't got much choice."

"I don't understand. Why now?"

"Things ain't like they was when I was growing up. Hell, even when *you* were a boy it was different." Sweetie watched a wasp struggling against the glass sliding door that led to the concrete patio in the backyard. Its bony body craved the warmth of the setting sun just on the other side. "Ain't no feuding between people like the Cranks and the Osbournes, just going out and dropping the hammer on someone. I need to keep busy doing what I've always done or I'm gonna end up shooting one of them boys dead."

"Those boys are a lot stouter than you are, Sweetie. Looking for trouble is a good way to get cold-cocked," Tim said.

"You're right. It ain't my business anyways. I go down there with that revolver and my fate is sealed. Either way, though, I reckon I sealed it a long time ago."

"You ain't sealed nothing. Just leave it be, Sweetie," Tim said.

Sweetie shook his head. He stepped on the insect and crushed its body into the corner where the floor and the bottom panel of the door met. He twisted his ankle so that the toe of his cowboy boot crunched out the wasp's last desperate fluttering.

"I wish I could. I pray I find the strength to do so. But I think it's already set in motion."

"A man needs more than five rounds for something like that. You might scare them away with a revolver, but you sure as hell ain't going to hit anything with it."

"By the time I squeezed off a couple, some kind of an end would be near. I don't know what I'm going to do," Sweetie said.

"Those types of things tend to happen fast." Tim wasn't taking him seriously. He was scratching something down in his notebook. He had it pinned down against the counter by his coffee cup. "You know me though, I'm a pacifist. 'Do violence to no man' is what John the Baptist told the soldiers. So how much you want?" Tim asked.

"I have a thousand dollars cash. However much that will get me."

Through the window, at the kitchen sink, clouds formed a wall across the entire horizon above the eastern hills. Sweetie could pick Turkeyfoot out of the mountains just by the shape of it. Billowing towers of clouds stained with pink, orange, and yellow rays of dusk hung above it. At their center was an opening like a bleeding gash, where the fading blue sky peered through. From Tim's marble countertops, the mountain ridge looked a world away even though he knew it was only a short drive.

"One lesson I learned long ago was to keep my personal life and this business separated. It saves a man a whole lot of trouble. I'd hate to see you do something you regret, Sweetie. You and I have made a lot of money together. We could make even more." For the first time in their conversation, Sweetie and Tim looked each other in the eyes.

CHAPTER FIFTY-SIX

Sweetie's truck sat idling. He shifted the vehicle into park but wasn't sure why he kept the ball of his foot pressed firmly against the brake pedal. The wide spot in the road was the same as always, only the stream seemed to flow a little slower off the slate rock. In the passenger seat next to him sat an empty gallon jug to fill for his father.

CHAPTER FIFTY-SEVEN

The nursing home smelled of sanitized death. He still considered it a holding place for old souls on their way out of this world, but the old man had lasted a lot longer than he ever expected. Sweetie signed his name on the visitor's log. A bulky bouquet sat in a vase next to his elbow on the counter. The girl behind the office window stared at him dumbly. Her name tag was pinned crooked to the top of her pink scrubs. Sweetie recognized another woman cleaning in the dining area. She glanced up and waved at him, smiling with her mouth closed, her lips deflated against her gums. He knew it was from having them pulled out for a prescription of pills. Half of which she shot up her arm and the other half she had sold to him for some quick Christmas money many years ago.

The hall to his father's room was narrow, the walls painted white and tan with a wooden handrail at waist height between the two colors. One woman pushed a cart from doorway to doorway. Her soft white sneakers squeaked as she shuttled across the waxed floor. Sweetie pardoned himself as he brushed past her, twisting his hips to avoid hitting her cart. When he stepped through to his father's room, he was surprised by how dark it was with the shades pulled shut. Shame stewed at the bottom of Sweetie's guts. His father slept with a heavy comforter pulled up to his chin. He stood at the foot of the bed watching the man who raised him struggle to take shallow breaths. Sweetie sat the gallon jug on a seat in the corner of the room.

"He can't have that here," the woman with the cart said standing at the door. "We have our own water. It's the city hookup. He's been drinking it just fine."

"He'll drink it, but that don't mean he likes it," Sweetie said.

"Well, he ain't got a choice. Visitors are only allowed to bring sealed items for the residents."

"Do whatever you want with it. I'm going to leave it here for him."

Sweetie walked around to his father's bedside. He leaned over and kissed the man on his forehead. The nurse moved on with her cart. Sweetie squeezed his father's hand in his grip before walking back out into the hallway where a lady sat in a wheelchair half asleep. A woman in a flowery blouse came and wheeled her back around towards a doorway on the other end of the hall. Sweetie put his head down, quickly walked through the lobby, and back out to his truck.

He pulled the revolver from underneath his seat and stared down the sights with both eyes open. He aimed it at a light on his dashboard. The snub nose's chrome body glistened even in the dark of his truck cab. His wrist tightened. His index finger hooked around the trigger. The hammer leaned back and snapped forward with a dull metal click. Sweetie swung the cylinder open and eyed the empty chambers. He shined the finish with the tail of his shirt and tucked the handgun back beneath his seat.

Back at home, he fixed dinner for himself. He sawed out a slab of cornbread and perched it atop a steaming bowl of soup beans. He ladled extra broth out over the cornbread and broke it up with the bottom of his spoon. Sweetie sprinkled salt over his bowl and could feel his mouth begin to water. He propped his feet up and spooned his dinner into his jaws. The furnace's fire crackled as it devoured green wood that had sat under spring showers.

Sweetie stripped down to nothing but his underwear and settled into sleep on the couch for the night. Outside his window gray hills steeped upward into the night. The universe screamed above, breathing cosmic winds out to the edge of eternity. Sweetie got up off the couch and walked to the porch. He stepped down into the yard. Blades of grass tickled his ankles and toes, the night air warm against his bare thighs. The stars stood sharp against the sheet of black that flattened out across the horizon.

CHAPTER FIFTY-EIGHT

Sweetie's phone woke him up on the first ring.

"They's some boys up here at Tuttle's Holler that want some dope." It took a moment for Case's words to snap together in Sweetie's head. The young man seemed to be holding his breath on the other side of the line.

"You got anything?" Case asked before Sweetie could respond. Sweetie turned his head to the clock on the wall that read well past midnight. It was nearly two in the morning.

"I ain't coming all the way out there to fool with y'all this late. Knowing you, I'll drive all the way up there and your dumbasses won't even have money."

"Oh, they got money. Bring all you got."

Sweetie pulled on clothes and a jacket and left the furnace burning.

Tuttle's Hollow lay at the bottom of a narrow dirt road that branched off from the main drag up Turkeyfoot, the way down uneven and steep. As soon as his front wheels dropped down over the edge of the pavement and met the gravel decline, he wondered what his odds of coming back up the hill were. The rain had worn a rut through the center of the road that forced Sweetie to straddle the bank with his truck tires so that he didn't drag his bottom out. He passed someone's old family grave plot on his way down, and when the road leveled out at the bottom the sky opened above. Stars spanned above the dips in the mountain ridge. Sweetie felt like he was staring up from the bottom of a water bucket. A field of hay stretched out across the hollow until the mountain and the trees climbed back up toward the sky.

A lone shack sat in a shallow curve off the mud road. Sweetie glared up for the moon, but it was too low to see down in the bottom. There wasn't an electric pole or a telephone line in sight. The place was pristine. His headlights beamed over Case and his brother standing out front of the small house. Tyvek paper hung loosely from the sides of the structure, the bottom of the wrap torn by dogs' teeth where it hung down towards the foundation. Sweetie's stomach turned at the sight of Case. He was tall and scrawny with long strands of hair flat over his bare shoulders, wearing a denim cutoff shirt that revealed a tattoo of a dragon spiraling up his bicep. Case moved his hands in wide circular motions while talking to his brother. The younger brother James was more compact, muscles traced up the length of his arms, and he stood with his hands stuffed in his jeans. The small house's door had long been kicked in. On the inside, painted initials and proclamations of love were smeared across its walls. Crushed cans were scattered about, and a faded cardboard beer box lay flattened on the ground. Case paced back and forth kicking up dirt with the toes of his boots. Sweetie pulled the front end of his truck around to face the sad little shack and the two men.

Sweetie let the truck idle; he cut his high beams on and lit half the bottom up. James turned and Case held up a hand to shield his eyes at first, then raised his head to look straight through the blinding headlights into the cab of the truck. Sweetie cut the engine and the natural sounds of the night filled his ears. Insects chirped, and even though the night was warm, a chilly breeze of air seemed to pass through his window.

Sweetie reached between his legs to the floorboard. His hand came to the Smith & Wesson. He pulled it out and checked the cylinder. He had loaded it before going to sleep, but now he pushed the wheel gun back underneath the seat and patted his boot for the bag of fentanyl from Tim. When he opened the door to step out, the cab light shone and the dashboard *ding, ding, dinged* before he pocketed the truck keys and swung the door closed again. The tree branches whistled on the hill. Somewhere across the field behind him that owl screeched. The ground was stiff beneath his heels as he stepped toward the cabin. The two younger men began to cross the road against him. Sweetie's eyes fell to Case's shrunken waist and pants cinched up tight with a leather belt that had extra holes punched through it. Case's fingers looked long and sharp in the shadows, his fingernails were glossy in the moonlight with thick grime beneath their tips.

"What y'all doing down here in the dark?" Sweetie called out.

The short stocky brother quickened his step and brought his left fist across Sweetie's jaw. Sweetie tripped backward and the man fell atop of him, bringing a forearm down into Sweetie's nose. Case began kicking the old man in the ribs again and again, raising a boot and stomping down on Sweetie's stomach. He stomped until a rib cracked and Sweetie breathed desperately in the dirt.

"He keeps it in his boot," James said to his brother.

The tall bony figure yanked and twisted at his freshly polished cowboy boot. Sweetie could feel his ankle strain and pop with each tug and twist. The cold damp earth was wet on Sweetie's back. He braced for each of James's blows and tried to shield his face from the gritting pair of teeth straddling his chest and lashing at his temples. Case finally got the boot off and the bag of fentanyl fell out to the ground. Case pitched the boot into the tree line out of sight, stepping on Sweetie's ankle and grinding it beneath his heel.

"Now that's a fucking score! Where're his keys at?!" Case yelled.

Sweetie's eyes went to the sky. The moon was still

somewhere low behind the mountaintops and the sun wouldn't rise for a long time yet. The boys rolled him over and ripped his coat off his back, Case fingering each pocket until he found the keys. Despite every kick and blow, Sweetie could only feel his mouth drying out. James rolled the old man over into the ditch line and the two brothers loaded into the Silverado. Case Estes gunned the engine, spinning wheels and slinging gravel as they left Sweetie to die at the bottom of the holler. Sweetie's rib cage began to throb with each breath. He wanted nothing more than one last taste of that Turkeyfoot spring water trickling just around the bend.

CHAPTER FIFTY-NINE

Lucy's bare feet pitter-pattered as they slapped across the kitchen tiles. She stood in the doorframe of the living room; her toes pressed down into the coarse carpet with her heels cold against the tile behind her. Her father was picking through cigarette butts and emptying them into a pile on the coffee table so that he could roll what tobacco was left into something smokable.

"Hey there, bright eyes," he said looking up from the Marlboro filters and ash spilled like guts. A thin blanket was neatly folded at one end of the couch. A thinner pillow was stuffed behind him.

"I want some breakfast," Lucy said. She rubbed the crust from her eyes with her small fists.

"You want me to scramble you some eggs?" John had shifted his attention back to his desperate operation. The front door was propped open with a boot, allowing a little bit of spring breeze to make its way into the living room.

"I don't want eggs. I want to go to Dairy Queen."

"We ain't got money to be buying Dairy Queen. I have to find a way to pay this electric bill today. You better let me make you some eggs while the stove still works."

"I don't want eggs," Lucy said.

John's entire body was aching for a cigarette. He had been smoking more often after trying to kick the pill habit, but even cigarettes weren't cheap. He finally had enough tobacco piled to crudely roll a cigarette. He lit it and took a deep drag. His loosely rolled abomination burned faster than a sparkler the day after Fourth of July, and within a few minutes there wasn't even any smoke lingering in the room.

"I'm sorry, honey. Eggs are all I got for you." John had peered into the empty fridge enough times already this morning. They had four eggs, a couple of cans of soda, and the same half-eaten jar of pickled bologna that had probably earned squatting rights at that point.

John had been trying to land another factory job, but he wasn't having any luck. The temp agency would call, and he may have some work for a few weeks before the place said they didn't need him anymore. He refused to go back to the mill to work for Tim. He knew that to do so would be the same as giving up on his newfound sobriety given the crew and Tim's own workplace incentives.

Lucy watched as her father stood up from his place on

the broken-down couch and walked by her, completely ignoring what she had said about the eggs. He walked into the back bedroom. On top of a dresser sat Anne's wooden jewelry box. Four tiny drawers were stacked on top of one another on one side. The other half had a small glass door that swung open. The man grabbed the box and took it into the living room where Lucy sat in the middle of the stained carpet staring at the local morning news anchor whose face was stretched out into an artificial smile. The anchor was talking about a house that had burned down overnight, his waxy facial features made it seem as though he might melt into a puddle just talking about the fire.

John sat the jewelry box on the coffee table next to the mess of ash he'd made and opened the small glass door. He fingered through gold necklaces and bracelets hanging inside, picking a couple up and laying them out neatly on the table. Even with the sun shining in through the front door, the necklaces seemed as flat and dim as the wooden surface they rested on. John turned his attention to the drawers. He picked out a pallbearer's flower from his wife's funeral. It was cloth so it hadn't wilted, just faded in the months that had passed. He tossed it to the side with the rest of the items a pawnshop wouldn't be interested in, then plucked up a knot of rings and grazed through them.

After a few minutes, he sat back and looked over what he had. Most of it was junk. He knew that some of the gold would be his best bet; none of the rings had any diamonds or jewels worth anything. There was a herringbone necklace he was confident would be worth something. He had traded for it with a friend of his years ago. The 14K stamped sharply next to the snap cemented the herringbone's value. Just to make sure he'd have enough, he pocketed a handful of promising rings as well.

"What are you doing with Mommy's jewelry?" Lucy asked.

"We're going to go get some money so we can pay this bill. Go put on your shoes."

Lucy picked out her favorite pair of flip-flops. John kicked the old work boot out of his way and slammed the door behind him.

The air was hot and thick from rain the past couple of days. The air-conditioning in the Honda didn't work so they rode with the windows down. The constant rush of air punching through the car sent Lucy's hair in a thousand different directions.

When Lucy rode with her father all she could ever really see was what was above her. She could see the sky and some treetops and the telephone poles, but everything sped by so fast it made her sick to her stomach. Instead, she watched the necklace her father had hung around his rearview mirror. It was a thin gold chain with a small cross pendant, with an even tinier Jesus suspended from that. This necklace wasn't for sale. She stared up at it swinging all about, bouncing around as her father busted gears through each curve.

Lucy and her father pulled into what looked to have once been a small gravel parking lot. Behind the pawnshop was a maze of chain-link fence dividing up a neighborhood of people not unlike themselves.

John put the car in park and killed the engine. This wasn't a place for window shoppers. Lucy couldn't tell if the lights were on inside or not. A thick layer of grime spread from where the first window started, over the glass door, and down to the end of the second window. Lights or no lights inside, on the outside a neon OPEN sign shone as plain as day.

"I'll be right back, okay?" John took the key from the ignition and climbed up out of the cramped vehicle.

"I want to come in," Lucy said.

"The last thing we need is for you to get in here and break something. Just wait here." He lingered at the door for a second waiting for her to protest then slammed it together firmly. John started toward the store, keeping his boots as clean as possible, each step dodging mud puddles and potholes.

As soon as John stepped inside, a mustiness put him in a choke hold. There were piles of junk everywhere. On one stand was a rat's nest of different wires and cables with no telling what they went to. A rack in a corner was full of cheap guitars just waiting for some poor kid with more heart than money to come in and get his hopes up, only for the neck to come unseated in a week. Brand-name laundry detergent was stockpiled along the back wall and towers of soda crowded almost every aisle.

Behind the counter stood a plump, balding man. He stared at John over a pair of glasses that were on the verge of sliding off his sweaty face.

"Hey there," John said, approaching the man with confidence and pulling the herringbone out of his pocket. "I was hoping to sell you a little bit of gold this morning."

The man behind the counter glanced down at the necklace sprawled out before him with unimpressed eyes.

"Alrighty then. Let me have a look," the broker said.

He picked the necklace up and looked it over carefully, still not showing much interest. The fat man turned around and walked through a door to the back of the shop. John glanced around at what the pawnshop had behind its glass counter. Countless knives and old coins rested on the inside in rows and columns, all labeled, and much more organized than the rest of the place. He touched the rings in his pocket and wondered if he should have gone ahead and given them to the man, when the short stubby figure emerged again.

"It's plated." The man behind the counter tossed the necklace down on the counter in front of John Perley.

"It's what?"

"Plated. I don't even want to make you an offer, buddy. Sorry."

They stared at each other for a few seconds. John could smell cigar smoke coming from the back room. The odor was heavier than he was used to.

"Can you give me anything for these?" He pulled his wife's rings out, handing them to the man who eyed each one and again took off to the back of the shop.

"Sorry bastard." John stared down at the necklace still lying on the counter. The man came waddling back through the doorway.

"I'd offer you twenty bucks for this one, just because I think my wife might like it."

"Well, what about the other two?"

"I don't want the other two."

John cracked a smile and nodded his head at the response. It wasn't a crooked smile like the broker might have once he left. There was something solid in it; about as solid as John's broken and smoke-stained smile could muster.

Outside Lucy monkeyed with one of the vents on her side of the car, opening and closing it. She tried to fight her seatbelt and sit up enough to see what was going on around her, but she couldn't see the way her father came walking out of the shop. He didn't have the same strut he'd had walking in. When he opened the door and squeezed his long legs under the steering wheel, he was smiling at her.

"I'm gonna drive up here to this gas station to buy some cigarettes and then we'll go get some breakfast from Dairy Queen. Sound good, sweetheart?"

"Can I get an orange juice too?" Lucy asked.

John spent the night sitting at the foot of his bed. He hadn't slept in the room since Anne died, but he had taken some of her favorite clothes from the closet and spread them out neatly on the mattress. At first, he had traced their seams with his fingertip, then he buried his face in her favorite Kentucky Wildcats sweater. He inhaled deeply, desperate to pull out every last trace of her fading scent.

After he had everything out of the closet, he took it outside and stuffed the clothes into his burn barrel, a 55-gallon steel drum where he burned some of their trash and all of their cardboard. He doused the whole pile in kerosene and set it ablaze. It threw a great orange glow against the damp night.

John wondered if Lucy was okay in her room while flames caressed the rusted edges of the barrel. He figured she was fine. She was probably sleeping or playing with her toys. He knew she took care of herself. She had always been tough like that.

CHAPTER SIXTY

Over Lucy's head, the stars dribbled across the sky in streaks. The splattered streams of light ran from cluster to cluster. The dippers' frames stood rigid amongst it all. Lucy had snuck out the front door when she saw her father getting kerosene from the shed. She wished he hadn't burned her mother's clothes. She would've loved to have worn those old sweaters. Even if they didn't fit now, they would have one day. Lucy's naked feet skittered across the gravel and down the grassy yard to the embankment below their driveway. She had always played at the creek, but since seeing the elk it had become the only place that gave her hope. She dipped her toes into the trickling creek. The cold water took her breath away.

Lucy buried her feet deep in the creek silt. She dug her toes down deep, straining her ankles until the grit started to scratch the skin off the top of her feet. Her blood washed away in the cool spring water and swirled in clouds until it lost its color altogether and simply flowed away, past the bend, and down the hills, somewhere into a river greater than she could imagine. Lucy laid back and took it all in. The blossoming treetops spiderwebbed out across the dark sky above. Her chest filled with the cool air around her, like her young lungs directly inhaled the night clouds. She could feel a pebble digging into her shoulder, but she didn't dare move and lose that moment. Lucy had faith, just as her parents once had, that the little creek bed out past the edge of their yard would wash across this hill for eternity. And even as the years burned away, Lucy knew her footprints would never leave this place. The blue of the morning had begun to turn gold.

ACKNOWLEDGMENTS

First I would like to thank the Lord above for the ability to tell this story in the first place. I have had so many amazing people in my life who have supported me along this journey. Thank you to my wife, Sydni, for listening to me ramble about this dream for so long. All of my family, especially my loving parents Richard and Pamela Childers, for many sacrifices made and long hours worked. My granny Diane and papaw Oscar for always being there for me. I would never have come this far if it were not for Crystal Wilkinson and Silas House, the two of you cracked this world of literature wide open for me. I was just writing stories about the stuff I knew, but y'all lit a fire under me. I can never thank you enough for your wisdom, guidance, and kindness. Thank you to all of the wonderful teachers and mentors I've had: Anne, Libby, Marie, Michael, Julie, Kirby, Wiley, Robin, Angela, David, and Michael. Thank you to Susan Berla for being a great writing partner who gave me crucial feedback in the early stages of this novel. As well as the Parsons bunch for their help and dedication to this story. I am grateful to all of my peers who have workshopped this project over the years. Shout out to the amazing writing communities at Berea College, the Loyal Jones Appalachian Center, the Southern Appalachian Writers Cooperative, the Naslund-Mann Graduate School of Writing at Spalding University, and the Appalachian Writers' Workshop at Hindman Settlement School. Lastly, thank you to Shotgun Honey and Ron Earl Phillips for lifting up the voices of Lucy and Sweetie.

RICK CHILDERS is a writer from Estill County, Kentucky. He received his BA in English from Berea College and an MA in Writing from the Naslund-Mann Graduate School of Writing at Spalding University. He also serves as Berea College's Appalachian Male Advocate and Mentor. His work has appeared in *Limestone Journal* as the runner-up for the Gurney Norman Prize for Fiction, *Pine Mountain Sand & Gravel*, *Still: the Journal*, *Heartwood Literary Magazine*, and the *San Joaquin Review Online*. He can be found on Facebook, Twitter, or at linktr.ee/rickchilders.

ABOUT SHOTGUN HONEY BOOKS

Thank you for reading *Turkeyfoot* by Rick Childers.

Shotgun Honey began as a crime genre flash fiction webzine in 2011 created as a venue for new and established writers to experiment in the confines of a mere 700 words. More than a decade later, Shotgun Honey still challenges writers with that storytelling task, but also provides opportunities to expand beyond through our book imprint and has since published anthologies, collections, novellas and novels by new and emerging authors.

We hope you have enjoyed this book. That you will share your experience, review and rate this title positively on your favorite book review sites and with your social media family and friends.

Visit ShotgunHoneyBooks.com

SHOTGUN HONEY

FICTION WITH A KICK

shotgunhoneybooks.com

Printed in the USA
CPSIA information can be obtained
at www.ICGtesting.com
LVHW030557011224
797960LV00011B/594